Friedrich Maximilian Klinger

Faustus

SALZWASSER
VERLAG

Friedrich Maximilian Klinger

Faustus

Reprint of the original, first published in 1864.

1st Edition 2022 | ISBN: 978-3-75259-196-5

Verlag (Publisher): Salzwasser Verlag GmbH, Zeilweg 44, 60439 Frankfurt, Deutschland
Vertretungsberechtigt (Authorized to represent): E. Roepke, Zeilweg 44, 60439 Frankfurt, Deutschland
Druck (Print): Books on Demand GmbH, In de Tarpen 42, 22848 Norderstedt, Deutschland

FAUSTUS:

HIS

LIFE, DEATH, AND DOOM.

A ROMANCE IN PROSE.

𝔗ranslated from the 𝔊erman.

"Speed thee, speed thee,
Liberty lead thee,
Many this night shall hearken and heed thee.
Far abroad,
Demi-god,
Who shall appal thee !
Javal, or devil, or what else we call thee."

LONDON

1864.

THE TRANSLATOR TO THE PUBLIC.

THE publication of the present volume may at first sight appear to require some brief explanation from the Translator, inasmuch as the character of the incidents may justify such an expectation on the part of the reader. It is therefore necessary to state, that although strange scenes of vice and crime are here exhibited, it is in the hope that they may serve as beacons, to guide the ignorant and unwary from the shoals on which they might otherwise be wrecked.

The work, when considered as a whole, is strictly moral. The Catholic priest is not praised for burning his fellow-creature at an *auto-da-fé*, and for wallowing in licentiousness; nor is the Calvinist commended for his unrelenting malignity to all those whose tenets are different from his own, and for crying down the most innocent pleasures and relaxations which a bountiful and just God has been pleased to place within the reach of his earthly children.

The tyrant and the oppressor of mankind will here find himself depicted in his proper colours.

Neither will the *champions of freedom* pass the fiery ordeal with feet unseared; since a glorious specimen of what they all are will be found among the following pages. Ye who with ever-open mouths are constantly clamouring at whatever is established, whether it be beneficial to the human race or injurious, will here find the motives for your conduct pointed out and held up to contempt and execration.

But, above all, this work contains the following highly useful advice:

Let every one bear his lot with patience, and not seek, at the expense of his repose, to penetrate into those secrets which the spirit of man, while dressed in the garb of mortality, cannot and must not unveil. Let every one bridle those emotions which the strange and frequently revolting phenomena of the moral world may cause to arise in his bosom, and beware of deciding upon them; for He alone who has power to check or permit them, can know how and why they happen, whither they tend, and what will be their ultimate consequence. To the mind of man all is dark; he is an enigma to himself: let him live, therefore, in the hope of once seeing clearly; and happy indeed is he who in this manner passes his days.

The present translation, it should be added, has been executed with as much fidelity to the original as the difference of the two languages, and other considerations, would allow.

CONTENTS.

CHAPTER I.

CHAPTER II.

CHAPTER III.

CHAPTER IV.

CHAPTER V.

FAUSTUS,

ETC.

CHAPTER I.

FAUSTUS, having long struggled with the shadows of Theology, the bubbles of Metaphysics, and the *ignes-fatui* of Morality, without being able to bring his mind to a firm conviction, at length cast himself into the dark fields of Magic, in the hope of forcing from Nature what she had so obstinately withheld from him. His first attainment was the remarkable invention of Printing; but his second was horrible. He discovered, almost fortuitously, the dreadful formula by which devils are called out of hell, and made subservient to the will of man. But as yet he had not exerted his power, out of love to his immortal soul, for whose welfare

every Christian is so anxious. At this period he
was in the full bloom of manhood. Nature had
favoured him in his person, and had given him
a noble and expressive countenance. Here was
enough to bespeak his happiness in the world; but
she superadded pride and untamable impetuosity
of mind, which displayed itself in deep determination of purpose, and in the constant workings
of a heated imagination, which was never satisfied
with the present, but affected to discover the empti-
ness and insufficiency of the acquired object, even
in the zest of its enjoyment.

Faustus soon lost the path by which modera-
tion leads frail mortals to the abode of true happiness. He soon felt the narrow limits of humanity,
and endeavoured to burst their bonds. By what
he had learnt and believed in his youth, he entertained a high opinion of the capacity and moral
worth of man; and, in comparing himself with
others, he naturally laid the greatest part of the
sum-total to his own account. Here were fine
materials for greatness and glory: but true greatness and true glory generally fly from him who is

on the point of attaining them, just before he can
separate their fine pure forms from the mist and
vapour which delusion has shed round them. It
appeared to Faustus that, in his situation, the
nearest and most convenient way to honour and
. reputation would be the sciences; yet scarcely
had he tasted their enchantment when his soul
became inflamed with an ardent passion after
. truth. Every one who is acquainted with these
sirens, and has heard their deceitful song, must
know that, provided he does not make a mere
trade of them, he must infallibly miss his aim,
from the necessity of assuaging the burning thirst
with which they inspire him. Faustus, after he
had for a long time groped about in the labyrinth,
found that his earnings were doubt; displeasure
at the short-sightedness of man; and discontent
and murmuring against the Being who had formed
him. He might still have been comparatively
happy had he had only these feelings to combat:
but when the perusal of the sages and the poets
awakened a thousand new wants in his soul, and
his now winged and artificial imagination con-

jured up before his eyes the many intoxicating
enjoyments which gold and reputation could only
procure him, his blood ran like fire through his
veins, and all his faculties were soon swallowed up
by this sensation.

By the discovery of Printing, Faustus thought
he had at length opened the door to riches, honour,
and enjoyment. He exerted himself to the utmost, in order to bring the art to perfection, and
he now laid his discovery before mankind; but
their lukewarmness quickly convinced him that,
although the greatest inventor of his age, he and
his family would soon perish with hunger unless
his genius continually displayed itself in some
new forms. Hurled from the pinnacle of hope,
oppressed by heavy debts,—which he had incurred
by generosity and extravagant living, and by his
becoming security for false friends,—he now surveyed the world through a gloomy medium. His
domestic ties, when he no longer knew how to
support his family, became an intolerable burden.
He began to think that there was a malign influence in the distribution of men's fortunes: or

how did it happen that the noble and intellectual man was every where oppressed, neglected, and in misery; whilst the knave and the fool were rich, prosperous, and honoured in life?

In this melancholy state of mind Faustus wandered from Mayence to Frankfort, intending to sell one of his printed Latin Bibles to the magistracy, and then to return and buy with the produce food for his hungry children. He had been able to accomplish nothing in his native city, because at that time the Archbishop was at war with the whole Chapter, and all Mayence found itself in the greatest confusion. The cause was as follows: a Dominican monk had dreamt that he passed the night with his penitent, the lovely Clara, who was a white nun, and a niece of the Archbishop. In the morning it was his turn to read mass; he did so, and, unabsolved from the night of sin, received the host in his profane hands. At eve-tide, after a cup or two of Rhenish, he related his dream to a young novice. The dream tickled the imagination of the novice: he told it with some additions to a monk; and in

this manner the story, embellished with horrors
and licentiousness, ran through the convent, until
it came to the ears of the Prior himself. This holy
man, who hated Father Gebhardt on account of
his intimacy with the most respectable houses, was
shocked at the scandalousness of the affair, which
he considered as a profanation of the holy sacra-
ment; and, refusing to decide on such a weighty
matter, he referred it to the Archbishop. The
Archbishop, wisely concluding that whatever sinful man wishes or thinks by day he dreams of by
night, denounced the ban of the Church against
the monk. The Chapter, whose hatred to an Archbishop always increases the longer he lives, and
gladly seizes every opportunity to annoy him,
took Father Gebhardt under its protection, and
opposed the ban on these grounds : " It is well
known that the Devil tempted St. Anthony with
the most licentious representations and voluptuous
enticements; and if the Devil dared to act so with
a saint, whose equal was not to be found in the
calendar, what should prevent him from playing
off his pranks with a Dominican? We must there-

fore advise the monk to follow the example of the
holy Anthony, and, like him, to oppose the temptations of the fiend with the weapons of prayer and
fasting. It is, however, much to be lamented,
that Satan should have so little respect for the
Archbishop as to make the instrument of his wiles
assume the figure of one of his reverence's family."
The Chapter conducted itself in this case exactly
in the same manner as hereditary princes do
whose fathers live too long. But what served
more completely to confuse the case was a report
from the nunnery. The nuns had assembled in
the refectory, and were busied in dressing up a
Madonna for the next festival, hoping to surpass
by its magnificence their rivals the black nuns,
when suddenly the old porteress entered, told the
licentious story, and added, that the Dominican,
whose name she had forgot, would certainly be
burnt alive, for that the Chapter had even then
assembled for the purpose of trying him. Whilst
the porteress was relating the tale with its various
circumstances, the faces of the young nuns were
violently flushed, and Sin, who never loses an op-

portunity of corrupting innocent hearts, shot into
their blood, and hastily pictured the dangerous
scene to their imaginations. Fury and consterna-
tion, in the mean time, deformed the features of
the old ones. The abbess trembled and leaned on
her staff, while the spectacles fell from her face.
But when the porteress added, that it was the sister Clara whom the fiend had brought to the Dominican in his dream, a dreadful shriek filled the
whole hall. Clara alone remained tranquil, and
when the uproar had ceased, she said, smiling:
" Dear sisters, why do you shriek so fearfully? I
myself dreamt that I passed the night with Father Gebhardt, my confessor; and if it was the
work of the fiend" (here she and all the rest made
the sign of the cross), " why, we must give him the
discipline." " The Father Gebhardt!" cried the
porteress; "now, all ye saints and angels, that is
the very person who dreamt of you; that is he
whom they are about to burn." The porteress
having thus expressed herself, this second version
of the dream was immediately circulated through
the city. The Madonna was allowed to remain

naked, for the sisters cared now very little if the black nuns bore away the palm. The abbess did all in her power to spread the news abroad, the housekeeper followed her example, the porteress harangued an audience beneath the gateway, and Clara candidly replied to the yet more candid questions of her companions. The last trumpet could not have diffused in Mayence more terror and confusion than did this extraordinary tale.

No sooner did the Dominican prior hear of this accident than he ran to the assembled Chapter, and gave, by his information, a new turn to the affair. The Archbishop would willingly have suppressed the whole business; but it was now time for the Chapter to take it up, and all the canons were unanimously of opinion, that so strange a circumstance ought to be communicated to the Holy Father at Rome. They now became infuriated, and nothing but the midday bell had power to separate them. From that moment, all Mayence, clergy and laity, divided into two parties; and for many years nothing was heard, spoken, or dreamt of, but the Devil, the white nun, and Father Gebhardt. The matter was argued from the pulpit of every sect: mountebanks, Capuchins, and dog-doctors, made it their theme; while the lawyers, after having taken the depositions of the nun and the father, and confronted them with each other, wrote folio volumes concerning the sinful and unsinful chances of the dream. Was this a time for Faustus and his discoveries to succeed?

In Frankfort, which is at the present day the asylum of science, Faustus, however, hoped for better fortune. He offered his Bible to the reverend Town Council for two hundred gold guilders; but, as a large sum had just been expended in purchasing five hogsheads of prime Rhenish for the council cellar, his demand came rather unseasonably. He paid his court to the town-clerk, to the speaker, and to the senators,—from the proud patrician to the yet prouder head of the shoemaker guild. He was promised by all favour, protection, and assistance.

At length he attached himself to the then presiding mayor, from whom he for a long time gained nothing; but, as if in recompense, the lady-

mayoress kindled a violent passion in his suscep-
tible heart. One evening the mayor assured him
that the council, on their next day of meeting,
would come to a determination, by virtue of which
the assembled members would most probably pay
down the sum for the Bible. Faustus replied,
that his children might very possibly die of hunger before so enlightened an assembly had de-
cided; and, maddened with despair, he now
returned to his solitary apartment. In this moment he suddenly recollected his magic formula.
The thought of running some bold risk, and of
purchasing independence of man by an alliance
with the Devil, rushed more vividly than ever
through his brain. Yet the idea terrified him.
With hasty steps, furious gestures, and fearful
cries, he strode up and down the chamber, struggling with his rebellious spirit, which urged him
to penetrate the surrounding darkness; still his
soul shuddered and was unresolved. The clock
struck eleven from the neighbouring tower. Black
night hung about the earth. The north-wind
howled, and clouds obscured the face of the full

moon. Nature now appeared in a second chaos. A night more suited to bewilder an excited imagination could not be conceived. Yet was the beam of his mind balanced. In one scale hung religion and its firm supporter—the hope of immortality; while thirst for independence and knowledge, pride, pleasure, malevolence, and bitterness filled the other.

At length Faustus, according to the custom of magic, drew the horrible circle which was for ever to remove him from the providential care of the Omnipotent, and from the sweet ties of humanity. His eyes sparkled, his heart beat louder, and his yellow tresses stood erect on his head. At this moment he thought he saw his aged father and his blooming wife and children wring their hands in despair, and fall down upon their knees to pray for him to that Being whom he was about to renounce. "It is their misery, it is their situation, that maddens me," he wildly shrieked, and stamped on the ground with his foot. He now became enraged at the weakness of his heart, and advanced towards the circle; the storm rattled

against the windows, the foundation of the house
trembled : a noble angelic figure appeared before
him, exclaiming, "Stay, Faustus!" and the following colloquy ensued :

Faustus. Who art thou, that disturbest my
daring work ?

Figure. I am the Genius of Man, and will save
thee, if thou art to be saved.

Faustus. What canst thou give me to assuage
my thirst for knowledge, and my desire for freedom and enjoyment ?

Figure. Humility, resignation in suffering, content, and a proper estimation of thyself; above all,
an easy death, and light in the world to come.

Faustus. Begone, vision of my heated fancy!
I know thee by the cunning with which thou
wouldst deceive the wretches whom thou hast
made subservient to power. Begone, and hover
around the brows of the beggar, of the monk, of
the debased slave, and of all those who have their
hearts fettered by unnatural bonds ; and who keep
their senses locked up, in order to escape from the
claws of despair. The powers of my soul require

room, and let Him who has given me it answer
for its workings.

"Farewell, unhappy man," sighed the Genius,
and disappeared.

Faustus cried, "Am I to be frightened on the
very brink of hell by nursery-tales? But they
shall not prevent me from piercing the darkness;
I will know what the gloomy curtain conceals,
which a tyrannical hand has drawn before our
eyes. And who is to blame, I repeat? Was it I
that formed myself so that trifling exertion ex-
hausts my strength? Did I plant in my bosom
the seeds of passion? Did I place there that impulse for aggrandisement which never lets me
rest? Did I fashion my soul, so that it will not
submit, and will not bear contempt? Perhaps I
am like the earthen pot, which, formed by a strange
hand, is broken into pieces, because it does not hit
the fancy of the maker, and because it does not
answer the use for which it appears to have been
designed. Alas! I am a mere vessel; yet wherefore then this struggle with my destiny, which
would fetter my noblest resolves? And was mind

given for no purpose? Surely not! The bull trusts
in his horns, and the stag in his swiftness to escape
from the hunter; and is that which so eminently
distinguishes man less his own? Mind I possess;
I employed it for the benefit of my fellow-men,
and neglect was my reward; perhaps the devils
will respect it more."

Here he sprung furiously into the circle; while
the lamentations of his wife, father, and children
seemed to echo, in the deep tones of despair,
"Lost! for ever lost!"

Satan, ruler of hell, had, by the hoarse sound
of his trumpets, which echoed even to the glowing
sides of the sun, announced to all the fallen spirits
dispersed through the upper and lower world, that
he intended on this day to give a great festival.
The spirits assembled at the mighty call. Even
his envoys at the papal stool, and at the different
courts of Europe, forsook their posts; for the invitation led them to expect something great and
important.

Already the monstrous vaults of hell resounded
with the wild cries of the fiendish populace, while

myriads seated themselves upon the scorched
ground. The princes then stepped forth, and
commanded silence to the multitude, whilst Satan
heard the intelligence brought by his envoys from
the upper world. The devils obeyed, and a death-
like stillness prevailed amid the thick, misty darkness, interrupted only by the groans of the damned.
In the mean time the slaves of the fiends—shades
who are neither worthy of happiness nor damnation—prepared the immeasurable tables for the
banquet; and they deserved to be under the thral-
dom of such a task. When they were yet in flesh
and blood, and ate the fruits of the earth, they
were of that equivocal kind, who seem the friends
of all men and yet are the friends of none; whose
tongues continually prattle of the noble precepts
of virtue, which they feel not in their hearts; who
only abstain from evil because it is accompanied
by danger, and from doing good because it requires courage and self-denial; who traffic with
religion, and, like avaricious Jews, lay out their
capital at interest, for the purpose of securing a
comfortable berth for their miserable souls; and

who worship God from fear, and tremble before Him like slaves.

The devils, who, to say the truth, are no better masters than the Polish, Livonian, and Hungarian nobility, drove them about in hell at a furious rate. Others were sweating in the infernal kitchen, and cooking the meal for their haughty lords—an unpleasant service for a soul which had once supported its own human body by eating and drinking. For although the devils originally neither ate nor drank, yet they had learnt from men the custom of celebrating every solemnity by means of the glass and platter; and on such occasions they feast on souls. The general of each legion (for hell is arranged on a military footing, and in this respect resembles every despotic government, or rather every despotic government in this respect resembles hell) chooses a certain number of damned souls, as food for his subalterns. These are delivered over to the slaves, who stew, broil, and baste them with infernal sauce. It frequently happens that these wretches have to stick their own wives, daughters, fathers, sons,

or brothers upon the spits, and to keep up the pur-
gatorial fire beneath them; a truly horrible and
tragic employment, rendered yet more so, since
their overseer, a capricious devil, like all under-
strappers of great lords, stands behind them with
a whip in order to expedite the work. On the present occasion two popes, a conqueror, a celebrated
philosopher, and a recently canonised saint, were
intended to feast the palates of Satan, his viziers,
and his favourites. Abundance of fresh victuals
had just arrived for the common people. The
pope had a little time before set by the ears two
armies of French, Italians, Spaniards, and Germans, in order to fish up in the tumult certain
districts, to add to the patrimony of St. Peter.
They fought like heroes, and fell by thousands
into the infernal regions. What happiness would
it ·be for the souls intended for these devilish re-
pasts, if they were thereby to find an end to their
torments! But no sooner are they swallowed, di-
gested, and returned piecemeal into the pools of
hell than they are regenerated, and arise to become the patients of new suffering.

While these victims were writhing on the spits, the cellarers and butlers, slaves of the above-mentioned order, decked out the sideboards. The flasks were filled with tears of hypocrites, of would-be saints, of pretenders to sensibility, and of persons who repent from weakness of soul; with tears which envy squeezes out on hearing of another's prosperity; with tears of egotists who weep for joy because they themselves have escaped the misfortunes by which others are overwhelmed; and of sons who weep over the palls of their harsh and avaricious fathers. The flasks on the supper-table were filled with the tears of priests, who, like actors, play a part in the pulpit, in order to move their auditors; and to give the liquor a sharper flavour, it was mingled with tears of court-esans, who walk the streets weeping for hunger, until some inexperienced youth barters his dollar with them for sin. Reserved for Satan and his princes stood, on various sideboards, flasks of the noblest drink. This was heady and foaming, be-ing a mixture of the tears of monarchs, who weep for the misery of their subjects, whilst they issue commands only calculated to perpetuate it; of the tears of maidens who weep for the loss of their chastity with streaming eyes; and of the tears of favourites who have fallen into disgrace, and now weep because they can no longer rob and oppress under the protection of their masters.

No sooner had the slaves decked the table, and stationed themselves behind the chairs of their masters, than the grandees poured forth from the chambers of Satan. The furies went foremost; the body-guards followed them, and were succeeded by the chamberlains. Then came pages bearing lighted torches, woven out of the souls of monks who entrap wives, and press round the deathbed of husbands to force them to leave their property to the Church, without reflecting that their own illegitimate spawn must beg for bread through the land. Then came Satan himself, closely followed by the remaining nobility of his court, according to their rank and favour. The devils bowed their heads in reverence, the pages placed the torches upon the table of their sovereign; while Satan, with a triumphant air, mounted his high throne, and delivered the following speech:

"Princes, potentates, immortal spirits, welcome! thrice welcome! Rapturous emotions glow through me when I cast my eyes along your squadrons of countless heroes. We are yet what we were when, for the first time, we awoke in this pool from the stunning consequences of our fall, and for the first time assembled here. Only one feeling still rules,—unanimity alone maintains her sway, and in this place only do all devote themselves to the same end. He who has the happiness of commanding you may easily forget all other glory. I own we have suffered, and still suffer, much, especially since the full exercise of our powers is restrained. But in the feeling of the vengeance which we take on the sons of dust,—in the contemplation of their madness and crimes, by which they continually thwart the purposes of their being,—lies a recompense for our suffering. Welcome, thrice welcome, all ye whom this sentiment inflames.

"Hear now the occasion of the festival which

I intend this day to celebrate with you. Faustus,
a daring mortal, who, like us, is at war with the
Eternal, and who, through the strength of his
spirit, may at some future period be deemed worthy to dwell along with us here, has discovered
the art of multiplying, on an easy principle, a
thousand and a thousandfold, those things deno-
minated books,—those dangerous toys of men,—
those vehicles of delusion, of error, of lies, and
of horror,—those sources of pride and of painful
doubt. Until now they have been too costly, and
only in the hands of the rich, whom they filled
with fancies, and from whom they chased that
humility which God had for their happiness infused into their hearts. Triumph! Soon will
the poison of knowledge and inquiry be communicated to all classes. New cravings, new wants,
will arise; and I doubt whether my enormous
kingdom will be able to contain all those who will
destroy themselves by this delicious poison. But
this were only a slight victory: my eye pierces
deeper into that distant period, which is to us no
more than an hour is to man. Soon will cavillers

and haters of the established Church spread about
like the plague: pretended reformers of heaven
and earth will arise, and their doctrines, from the
facility of communication, will penetrate even into
the hut of the beggar. They will think to do
good, and to purify the object of their hope from
falsehood. But, if men begin well, how long do
they continue to act so! Sin is not more inseparable from them than are ill consequences from
their noblest pursuits. The well-beloved people
of God, whom he endeavoured to snatch from evil
by the sacrifice of his only Son, will quarrel about
tenets which no one understands, and will tear each
other to pieces like wild-beasts. Horrible atrocities, surpassing all the abominations perpetrated
by men since they first sprung into existence, will
desolate unhappy Europe. My hopes appear to
you too bold,—I read it in your doubting countenances; but listen to me whilst I explain. Religious disagreements will give rise to these frenzies.
Then first will Fanaticism, the wild son of Hatred
and Superstition, untie all the bonds of nature and
humanity. The father will murder the son, and

the son the father; kings will joyfully dip their
fingers in the blood of their subjects, and place the
sword in the hands of bigots, in order that they
may slaughter their brothers by thousands, because their opinions are different. Then will the
water of the rivers turn into streams of blood, and
the shrieks of the murdered will shake hell to its
very centre. We shall see wretches come down
to us stained with crimes for which we have had
hitherto neither names nor punishments. Already
do I see them attack the papal chair, which keeps
together the fragile fabric through treachery and
deceit, whilst it undermines itself through crime
and luxury. The great props of the religion
which we dread give way; and, if the sinking
structure be not sustained by means of new miracles, it will disappear from the face of the earth,
and we shall once more shine in the temples as
worshiped divinities. Where will the spirit of
man stop, when he has once undertaken to illumine that which he formerly honoured as a mystery? He will dance on the grave of the tyrant,
at whose frown he the day before trembled. He

will break to pieces the altar on which he lately
sacrificed, if he once endeavour to find the way to
heaven by his own wisdom. Will the Creator
take home to himself a human being, who is not
a million times more allied to us than to him?
Man abuses every thing, even the strength of his
soul as well as of his body. He abuses all that
he sees, hears, feels, or thinks; and all with which
he trifles, or with which he is seriously engaged.
Not content with deforming whatever he can seize
with his hands, he soars upon the wings of imagination into worlds to him unknown, and arrays
them in ideal deformity. Even freedom, the noblest of his treasures, to obtain which he has shed
rivers of blood, he readily sells for gold and pleasure, before he has tasted its sweets. Incapable of
good, he yet trembles at evil, he heaps horror
upon horror to escape it, and then destroys his
own handiwork.

"After the bloodshed of war, mankind, wea-
ried with slaughter, will take a few moments'
repose, and then their venomous hatred will be
displayed in petty and private bickerings. Some,

indeed, will every now and then raise piles of
wood and fagot, and burn those alive who dis-
agree with them in religion; others will attempt
the solution of inexplicable riddles; and those
born for darkness will dare to struggle for light;
their imaginations will become inflamed, and their
desires insatiable. Truth, simplicity, and religion
will be trodden under foot, for the sake of writing
a book. Yes, yes, book-writing will become a
universal employment, by which fools and men of
genius will alike seek fame and emolument; caring very little whether they confuse the heads of
their fellow-creatures, and hurl firebrands into
the hearts of the innocent. The heaven, the earth,
the secret strength of nature, the dark causes of
her phenomena, the power which rules the stars
and bowls the comets through space,—every thing
visible and invisible,—they will wish to handle,
measure, and dive into. They will invent, for all
that is incomprehensible, words and numbers;
and heap system upon system, till they have
brought deeper darkness upon the earth, through
which doubt, like the fen-fire, will only shine to

allure the wanderer into the morass. Only then
will they think to see clearly, and then I expect
them. After they have shovelled away religion,
and are forced, out of the remains, to patch together a new and monstrous mixture of human wisdom and superstition, then I expect them. And
then open wide the gates of hell, that the race of
man may enter. The first step is already taken;
the second is near. But this must be preceded by
a horrible revolution upon the face of the earth.
Soon will the inhabitants of the old world emi-
grate, for the purpose of discovering new, and to
them unknown, regions of the globe. They will
there attack and slaughter millions, to possess
themselves of that gold which the innocents value
not. They will fill this new world with all their
crimes, and then return with materials for corrupting even the old one. Thus will nations become our prey, whom till now innocence and
ignorance have protected from us. And thus
shall we, by the assistance of the favourites of
heaven, triumph.

"This, then, O potentates! is what I wished

to communicate to you; and now rejoice with me over this mighty day, and enjoy in anticipation the victory which I, who know men, promise you. Long live Faustus!"

With horrible uproar, which made the axis of the earth tremble, and the bones of the dead rattle in their coffins, the devils shouted, "Long live Faustus!" "Long live the corrupter of the sons of dust!" Hereupon the chief nobility of the kingdom were permitted to kiss the hand of his Satanic majesty.

The triumphant devils now sat down to table, and fell upon the prepared meal. The goblets clattered, the souls were craunched between their iron teeth; and they drank the health of Satan, of Faustus, of the clergy, of the tyrants of the earth, and of future and living authors, amidst the clang of hellish artillery. In order to render the banquet more magnificent, the masters of the revels went to the pools, drew out the burning souls, and chased them over the tables, to illumine the gloomy scene; while they ran behind the wretches with poisoned whips, forcing them to caper; and sparks ascended to the blackened roofs, crackling like wheat-sheaves ignited by lightning in an autumn storm. That the devils might have music to their meat, others hastened to the pools, and poured molten metal amid the flames, so that the damned howled and cursed in grisly despair. If priests now could, instead of their cold and fruitless sermons about penitence, give a specimen upon earth of these horrid cries, sinners would quickly turn a deaf ear to the voluptuous warblings of castrati, and join in some pious psalm: but, alas, hell is distant, and pleasure close at hand. After the banquet a great stage was erected, and various plays were performed, founded on the heroic deeds of Satan; for example, the Fall of Man, the Betrayal of Judas Iscariot, &c.

The performance was then suddenly changed to an allegorical ballet. The scene was a wild and dreary spot. In a dark cavern sat Metaphysics, in the shape of an Egyptian mummy, whose eyes were fixed upon five glittering words, which flitted continually backwards and forwards, and at each change had a different import. The

mummy ceased not to follow them with its stony
eyes; while in a corner stood a little roguish
devil, who incessantly blew bubbles of air into its
face. Pride, the amanuensis of Metaphysics, gathered the bubbles up as they fell, pressed the air
out, and kneaded them into hypotheses. The
mummy was clothed in an Egyptian waistcoat,
embroidered with mystic characters. Over this it
wore a Grecian mantle, which ought to have concealed the characters, but was much too short and
too narrow for that purpose. Its legs, thighs, and
body, were cased in long loose drawers, which
did not, however, entirely conceal its nakedness.
A huge doctorial hat covered its bald head, which
was marked with the scratches worn by its long
nails in provoking deep reflection. Its shoes were
made after the European fashion, and sprinkled
with the finest dust of the schools and universi-
ties. After it had gazed a considerable time on
the moving words, without being able to understand them, its attendant, Pride, gave the wink
to Delusion, who was walking near. He seized
a wooden trumpet, and sounded a dance. No

sooner did the mummy hear the noise than it took Pride by the hand, and danced about with antic gambols; but its thin withered legs could not bear this long, and it soon sunk breathless into its former posture.

Then came forward Morality, a fine female form, hooded in a veil, which, chameleon-like, sported all colours. She held Virtue and Vice by the hands, and danced a trio with them. For music, a naked savage played upon an oaten pipe, a European philosopher scraped the fiddle, while an Asiatic beat the drum; and although these contradictory tones would have distracted an harmonious ear, yet the dancers did not once lose the step,—so well had they learnt their parts. When the maiden gave Vice her hand, she coquetted and languished significantly before him; but when she gave it to Virtue, she moved along with the modest gait of a matron. After the dance, she reposed upon a thin, transparent, and beautifully-painted cloud, which her admirers had woven out of various shreds and remnants.

Next appeared nude Poetry: she danced with

Sensuality a characteristic dance, to which Imagination played the flute d'amour.

History then advanced upon the stage. Before her went Fame, with a long brazen trumpet. She herself was hung round with stories of murders, poisonings, perjuries, conspiracies, and other horrors. Behind her panted, beneath a prodigious load of chronicles, diplomas, and documents, a strong nervous man, clothed in the German fashion. She danced with Slavery, to the rustling of the stories with which she was hung. Falsehood at length took the trumpet from the mouth of Fame, and tuned it to the dance; and Flattery led the figures.

Then appeared Medicine and Quackery, and were received with loud laughter: they danced a minuet, to which Death clinked the music with a purse of gold.

After them were seen Astrology, Cabala, Theosophy, and Mysticism. They grasped each other by the hands, and whirled around in intricate figures; while Superstition, Delusion, and Fraud stood near, and blew the bagpipes.

These were followed by Jurisprudence, a sleek, rosy-faced dame, fed with fees, and hung about with commentaries—she coughed through a tedious solo; and Chicanery played the bass-viol.

Last of all entered Policy, in a triumphant car drawn by two mares, Weakness and Deceit. On her right sat Theology, holding in one hand a sharp-pointed dagger, and in the other a blazing torch. Policy herself wore a golden crown upon her head, and supported a sceptre over her right shoulder. She descended from the car, and danced with Theology a pas-de-deux, to which Cunning, Ambition, and Tyranny played on soft tinkling instruments. After she had finished the pas-de-deux, she made all the other figures a sign to begin a general dance. They immediately obeyed, and sprang about in wild confusion. All the before-mentioned musicians played on their instruments, and raised a din, only surpassed in loudness by the table-music of Satan. Yet Contention soon insinuated herself among the unsuspicious dancers; and, animated by Zeal and Fury, they hastily snatched up weapons. When Theo-

D

logy perceived that all embraced delightful Poetry, and that Morality wished to tear off her own veil, in order to cover her with it, she gave the latter a thrust with a poniard from behind, and singed the nude and tender Poetry with her flaming torch. Both raised a dreadful shriek: Policy commanded silence, and Quackery hastened to bind up the wound of Morality, whilst Medicine cut a shred from her robe in payment. Death stretched out his claw from under the mantle of thievish Medicine to seize Morality, but Policy gave him such a blow that he yelled aloud, and grinned most hideously. Poetry was allowed to hop about, because she was naked, and had nothing to be despoiled of. At length History took pity on her, and laid upon the burn a wet leaf from a sentimental romance. Policy then tied them all behind her chariot, and drove away in triumph.

All hell expressed approbation of this last spectacle by reiterated clappings; and Satan embraced the devil Leviathan for having got up the entertainment, which flattered him exceedingly, it being one of his chief whims to be reckoned by the fiends as the inventor of the sciences. He often said, in his pride, that he had begotten them in his intercourse with the daughters of earth, in order to divert men from the straightforward and noble feelings of their hearts; to remove from their eyes the mystic veil which constitutes their happiness; to make them acquainted with their state of restriction and weakness; and to fill them with painful doubt concerning their after destination. "I taught them," he would continue, "by their means, to reason, so that they might forget to practise virtue, and to worship. We ourselves have defied Heaven with bold and open weapons, and I have at least shown them the way of skirmishing incessantly with the Eternal."

The sensible reader will here pause, and admire the strict resemblance of all courts to each other: that is, how the great, through the service, toil, and sweat of the little, win the favour of their sovereigns, and bear away the rewards. Leviathan gave himself out as the inventor of this allegorical ballet, and was on that account thanked

and caressed, although the real author of it was
the Bavarian Poet Laureate, who a short time
before had died of hunger, and found his way to
hell. He prepared the .ballet after the latest
court-fashion, by the command of Prince Leviathan, who had at least talent enough to. discover merit: the reason of his bitter allusions to
the sciences was, probably, because they had so
ill supported him; and perhaps Leviathan, who
knew perfectly well what would please Satan, had
given him a hint to that effect. Be this as it
may, the devil had the reward, and the thin shade
of the Bavarian Laureate sat cowering behind a
rock of the theatre, and observed with bitterest
agony the marks of unmerited favour which Satan
had lavished on Leviathan.

The half-intoxicated devils now became so
clamorous as nearly to drown the howls of the
damned; when suddenly the powerful voice of
Faustus echoed from the upper world through
hell. He had at length surmounted every obstacle, and now summoned before him one of the
first princes of the kingdom of darkness.

Satan started up in ecstasy: "It is Faustus
who calls there. No one else has the power; and
no one else, if he had such power, would dare to
knock so loudly against the iron portals. Up!
up! a man like him is worth a thousand of the
scoundrels who come down hither every day by
rote." Then, turning to the devil Leviathan, his
favourite, he added, "I choose thee, the subtlest
seducer, the deadliest hater of the human race, to
ascend and purchase for me, by thy dangerous
services, the soul of this desperado. Only thou
canst chain, satiate, and then drive to despair, his
craving heart and his proud and restless spirit.
Quick, quick! ascend! dispel the vapours of
school-wisdom from his brain. Consume with the
fire of voluptuousness the noble feelings of his
heart. Disclose to him the treasures of nature,
and hurry him into life, that he may the sooner
grow tired of it. Let him see evil arise from
good, vice rewarded, justice and innocence trodden
under foot, as is the custom of men. Conduct him
through the wild and terrible scenes of human
life; let him mistake its aim, and lose among its

horrors the guiding thread of virtue. And when
he stands separated from all natural and heavenly
ties, in doubt concerning the noble destination of
his race,—when even pleasure and enjoyment have
left him, and the inward worm awakes,—then
depict to him, with infernal bitterness, the consequences of his deeds and delusions, and unfold to
him all their links, extending to remotest genera-
tions. If despair should then seize him, hurl him
down, and return in triumph to hell."

Leviathan. Wherefore, O Satan, dost thou im-
pose this work upon me? Thou knowest that
I have long ago had enough of men, and of their
playground,—the world. What is to be made
out of wretches who, as thou hast observed, have
strength neither for good nor evil? Gold, ambition, or pleasure, can quickly make rascals of
them, who have for a short period pursued the
phantom virtue; and if any one should move
boldly at first along the path of vice, he will be
driven back when half-way by the spectres of his
crazy imagination. If, indeed, it were a proud
hot-headed Spaniard, a revengeful assassinating

Italian, or even a wild lascivious Frenchman, whom you wanted me to catch—but a German, one of those thick-pated swine, who slavishly bend before rank, riches, and all the artificial distinctions of men, who believe that their lords and princes are made of superior materials to themselves, and have a right to dispose of them just as they please, either in fighting their own battles, or those of other sovereigns! Hast thou heard from them for centuries a single word of rebellion against tyranny, or of shedding blood for the rights of man? Not one of them has, as yet, come down to hell in glory; a proof that these people have no distinguished heads among them. Those are to my mind who wish to clear up every thing, who fight with the adamantine shield of individuality, against which all prejudices, earthly or heavenly, are shivered. Show me such a man who is willing to become great on earth at the expense of his soul, and I will immediately ascend.

Satan. Shall devils, O Leviathan, be blinded by prejudice, like the sons of dust? I tell thee,

the man after our own heart is born under that
district of heaven. He is one of those who, en-
dued by nature with hot and furious passions,
rebel against all the old-established customs of
society. When such a spirit tears its way through
these cobwebs, it resembles a flame, which, by its
own fury, speedily consumes the materials which
feed its lustre. He is one of those visionary philosophers who strive to seize, through imagination,
what is denied to cold understanding; and who, if
they are unsuccessful, laugh at all knowledge, and
make pleasure and enjoyment their gods. Away,
away, Leviathan! soon shall a fire break out in
Germany which will spread through all Europe.
Already is the germ of that delusion springing up
which shall endure for centuries. What the German has once caught, he will not easily let go.

The commanding voice of Faustus now resounded for the second time. Satan continued:

"Thou mayst know by this call that he is no
trembler. Hasten to him, for, if thou delayest,
perhaps he may doubt the strength of his charms,
and hell will lose the fruits of his temerity.

Truly, the fellow is such a genius, that I can almost overlook his origin."

The devil Leviathan angrily replied: "I swear, by the hot and foul pool of the damned, that the rebel shall one day blaspheme, and curse this and the hour of his birth."

He went away wrapt in a veil of smoke, and the fiends pursued him with loud huzzas.

Faustus stood within the magic circle, while his breast swelled with rage. For the third time he repeated the dreadful formula, in a voice that resembled thunder. The door suddenly flew open; a thick vapour hovered around the margin of the circle; he struck into it with his magic rod, and cried in triumph, "Unveil thyself, thou thing of darkness!" The vapour dispersed, and Faustus saw a tall figure concealed beneath a red mantle.

Faustus. Why this tedious disguise to one who wishes to see thee? Discover thyself to him, who fears thee not in whatever shape thou mayst appear.

The Devil flung back his mantle, and stood in a daring and majestic attitude before the circle.

His fiery eyes sparkled from beneath their black brows, between which malice, hatred, fury, agony, and scorn had formed themselves in thick folds. These furrows were sunk in a smooth, clear, high-arched forehead, which contrasted strangely with the fiendish marks between the eyes. A finely-formed aquiline nose inclined towards a mouth which seemed to have been framed only for the enjoyment of immortal things. He had the mien of a fallen angel, whose countenance was once illuminated by the Godhead, but which was now obscured by a gloomy veil.

Faustus (*in surprise*). Is man, then, every where at home? Who art thou?

Devil. I am a prince of hell, and come because thy mighty call compels me.

Faustus. A prince of hell under this mask; under the figure of a man! I wished for a fiend, and not one of my own race.

Devil. Perhaps, Faustus, we are most so when we resemble ye; at least, no mask suits us better. Besides, is it not your custom to conceal what ye are, and to appear what ye are not?

Faustus. Bitter enough, and yet true as bitter; for, if our outsides looked like our insides, we should not be very different from that which we imagine you to be; still, I expected to see thee more terrible, and even hoped that thy appearance would try the strength of my courage.

Devil. Thus do ye always imagine things contrary to what they are. Probably you expected a devil with horns and a cloven foot, as the cowardly age has depicted him. But since you have ceased to worship the powers of nature, they have forsaken you, and you can no longer conceive any thing great. If I were to stand before thee such as I really am,—my eyes threatening comets, my body a dark, hovering cloud, which shoots lightning from its gloom, in my hand the sword which I once brandished against the Avenger, and on my arm the ponderous shield which his thunder pierced,—thou wouldst become a heap of ashes in thy circle.

Faustus. But then I should at least see something great.

Devil. I might admire your courage; but

you are never more ridiculous than in these
would-be grand bursts of feeling, when you con-
trast the little you can embrace with the monstrous and great which are so high above you.
Thus may the worm measure the trampling ele-
phant, and reckon his weight in the moment
when it dies beneath his powerful foot.

Faustus. Mocker! and what, then, is the spirit
within me, which, if it once get fairly on the lad-
der, will mount from step to step into infinity?
What are its limits?

Devil. The length of your own nose. But,
if you called me out of hell merely for this chit-
chat, permit me to return for ever. I have long
known your inclination to prate about that which
you do not understand.

Faustus. Thy bitterness pleases me; it chimes
in with my humour, and I should like to be better
acquainted with thee. What is thy name?

Devil. Leviathan; which signifies *all*, for I
can do all.

Faustus. Hear the braggart! Are devils, then,
so boastful?

Devil. 'Twas said merely to do honour to the shape in which thou seest me : but words are vain. Set me to the proof. What dost thou require ?

Faustus. Require? What an indefinite word for a devil! If thou art what thou seemest, anticipate desires, and gratify them ere they become wishes.

Devil. The noble steed champs the bit in fury when curbed by a timid rider : how he then resembles the man who feels wings that could bear him into light, yet who is kept down in the dark abyss! Faustus, thou art one of those fiery spirits who are not contented with the scanty meal of knowledge which Omniscience has set before them. Great is thy strength, mighty is thy soul, and bold thy will; but the curse of finite reason lies upon thee, as it does upon all. Faustus, thou art as great as man can be.

Faustus. Masquerading fiend, return into hell; must thou, too, deceive us by flattery ?

Devil. Faustus, I am a spirit formed of flaming light; I saw the monstrous worlds arise out of nothing : thou art of dust, and of yesterday. Do I flatter thee ?

Faustus. And yet must thou serve me if I command.

Devil. For that I expect the approbation of hell, besides a reward; neither man nor devil will work for nothing.

Faustus. What reward dost thou expect?

Devil. To have that which animates thee; that which would make thee my equal if it had power.

Faustus. I were well off then, truly; yet, adept as thou art, thou knowest little of men, if thou doubtest the strength of one who has set himself free from the bonds which nature has drawn so tightly round our hearts. How gentle did they appear to me once, when the eye of my youth clothed men and the world in the pure colours of morning! 'Tis gone; dark is my horizon; I stand on the gloomy verge of eternity, and have broken through the laws which keep the human race in harmony.

Devil. What madness is this, Faustus? Harmony! does *she* rule the confused dance of life?

Faustus. Silence! I feel it perhaps for the last time; and perhaps look back for the last time upon the pleasant, joyous days of youth. How lamentable that man must awake from this dream of bliss; that the plant must shoot up, in order to wither away as a tree, or be felled! Ha, demon, smile; I was once happy. But let that be forgotten which can never be recalled. Yes, we have only strength when we pursue wickedness. But wherein am I great? If I were so, should I want thee? Go, cunning flatterer; thou wilt only make me feel my own littleness.

Devil. He who is capable of feeling where the shoe pinches him, and has courage enough to tear away the cause of it, is at least great so far. More I will not say, and woe to thee if I were to stimulate thee with words.

Faustus. Observe me now, and tell me what my spirit requires, but what I dare not utter.

At these words Faustus pointed to himself, then towards the heavens, and moved his magic staff towards the east and the west. He then continued, " Thou wast, when nothing ——- "

laid his hand upon his breast and forehead:
"Here is darkness; let it be dispelled."

Devil. Desperate man! full well I know thy
wish, and tremble, devil as I am, at thy boldness.

Faustus. Wretched spirit! thou shalt not
escape by this subterfuge. In my burning thirst
I would undertake to drink dry the deep sea, if I
hoped to find at its bottom what I sought. I am
thine, or another's: I yet stand where no devil
can penetrate. Faustus is yet his own master.

Devil. Thou wast so a few minutes since.
But thy lot was cast when thou enteredst this
circle. Whoever has looked me in the face turns
back in vain; and thus I leave thee.

Faustus. Thou shalt speak, and remove the
dark covering which conceals from me the world
of spirits. I will know the destination of man,
and the cause of moral evil in the world; I will
know wherefore virtue suffers, and vice is rewarded; I will know why we must purchase a
moment's enjoyment by years of agony and sorrow. Thou shalt disclose to me the source of
things, and the mysterious causes of the pheno-

mena of the physical and moral world. Thou
shalt make Him, who has arranged all, compre-
hensible to me—yes! even if the vivid lightnings,
which at this moment shoot from thy demon eyes,
were to stretch me lifeless in this circle of damnation. Dost thou think that I have summoned
thee merely for pleasure and gold? Any das-
tard may fill his belly, and satiate the desires of
the flesh. Thou tremblest! Have I more courage than thyself? What quaking devil has hell
vomited out? And thou callest thyself Leviathan, who canst do all! Away, away! thou art
no fiend, but a miserable thing like myself.

Devil. Madman! thou hast not yet felt, as I
have, the vindictiveness of the Avenger, the anticipation of which alone would make thee return
to dust, even if thou didst bear in thy bosom the
united strength of men from the first to the last
sinner. Urge me no further.

Faustus. I will, and am resolved.

Devil. Thou inspirest me with reverence and
pity.

Faustus. Obedience is all I require.

E

Devil. Go to war with him who has lighted up a torch within thee which will consume thee, if fear do not extinguish it.

Faustus. I have done so, and in vain. Obey!

Devil. Insatiable man! But know that a devil has his bounds too. Since our fall, we have lost the idea of these sublime secrets, and forget even the language to express them. The pure spirits of yonder world can alone sing and imagine them.

Faustus. Dost thou think by this crafty excuse to cheat me of that which I desire?

Devil. Fool! I would wish for no better revenge upon thee than to be able to paint to thy soul, in the glittering colours of Paradise, all that thou hast lost, and then see thee writhe in despair. Knew I more than I know, can the tongue formed of flesh make intelligible to the ear of flesh what lies beyond the bounds of sense, and the disembodied spirit only comprehends?

Faustus. Then be a spirit, and speak! Shake off this figure.

Devil. Wilt thou then understand me?

Faustus. Shake off this figure, and let me see thee as a spirit.

Devil. Thy words are folly. Now, then, see me : I shall exist, but not for thee; I shall speak, but thou wilt not catch my meaning.

Leviathan then melted into a thin clear flame, and disappeared.

Faustus. Speak, and unfold the enigma.

As the soft west wind moves along the perfumed meadows and gently kisses the tender flowers, so did it murmur around the ears of Faustus. Then the murmur changed to a loud continued tumult, which resembled the rolling of thunder, or the dash of a breaker against the coral reef, or its howl and bellow in the caves of the ocean. Faustus crept close within his circle, and with difficulty supported himself.

Faustus. Ah, if this be the language of spirits, my dream has vanished; I am deceived, and must gnash my teeth in darkness. I have, then, exchanged my soul for the gratification of earthly lust! for that is all in which this intriguing devil can assist me. That is all against which I

risked eternity! I thought to move among men
enlightened as no one had ever yet been, and to
dazzle them with my glory like the rising sun.
The sublime thought of living for ever as the
greatest in their hearts is gone; and I am more
wretched than I was. Where art thou, trickster,
that I may vent my fury upon thee?

Devil (in his former figure). Here I am. I
spoke, and thou didst not understand the sense of
my words. Dost thou not feel that thou art born
for darkness? Thou canst not become that which
thou must not. Withdraw thy mind from im-
possibilities, and direct it to what is attainable.
Thou wishedst to hear the language of spirits;
thou heardst it, and wert stunned and deafened
by the sound.

Faustus. Provoke but my wrath, and I will
bruise thee to tears with my magic rod. I will
chain thee to the rim of my circle, and then stamp
on thy neck.

Devil. Do it, and hell will laugh at thy anger.
For every tear thou makest me shed, Despair
shall one day wring a drop of blood from thy

brow, and Revenge shall hold the scales to catch
and weigh it.

Faustus. How revolting to a noble creature
like myself to hold converse with an outcast, who
has only sense for wickedness, and will only assist
in wickedness!

Devil. How disgusting to be forced to listen
to a man who reproaches the Devil because he is a
devil, and does not boast of that shadow, Virtue,
like one of you!

Faustus. Vain boast. If thou couldst but taste
the moral value of man, by which he approaches
the immortal, and which makes him worthy of
immortality!

Devil. I can prove that it does not exist.

Faustus. Yes; I believe thou canst. And so
can any one of us who makes the measure of his
own wickedness that of all mankind, and who
makes that virtue contemptible which he has
never felt in his breast. We have had philosophers who in this matter have long had the start
of the Devil.

Devil. Better if thou hadst never read them;

thy head would then have been more clear, and thy heart more sound.

Faustus. Damnation! Is the Devil always right?

Devil. I will show you that which those philosophers only talk of. I will blow away from your eyes the clouds which pride, vanity, and self-love have collected, and so charmingly coloured.

Faustus. How wilt thou accomplish that?

Devil. By conducting thee through the theatre of the world, and showing thee men in their nakedness. Let us travel by water, by land, on foot, on horseback, on the rapid winds, and see the race of man. Perhaps we may discover that for which so many thousand adventurers have broken their necks.

Faustus. Agreed. Let us go through the world; I must intoxicate myself by variety and enjoyment; and I have long wished for a broader sphere of observation than my own wild heart. Let us go forth, and I will force the Devil to believe in human virtue. He shall avow to me that man is the eye-apple of Him whom I now no more must name.

Devil. Then will I return to hell a convicted liar, and give thee back the bond which thou wilt presently sign with thy blood.

Faustus. But if I were to trust a devil, who might palm upon me his own fiendish performances for the works of men, how would the scoffer laugh?

Devil. Such a monkish notion I should not have expected from one who has so long toyed with philosophy; but in this ye are all alike, fools and wise men. If any thing goes wrong, pride and self-love will never permit you to lay the blame on yourselves. Observe now those two words, Good and Evil, which you would fain stamp into ideas; for when you have words, you always think you have coined the empty sound into a thought. You labour with your eyes closed, and when you open them it is but natural that the good should be your own work, and the evil that of the Devil. Thus, then, must we poor devils ride about day and night, in order to turn to this or that piece of roguery the heart or the imagination of this or that scoundrel, who, if it had not been for us, would have remained an honest fellow. Faustus! Faustus! man seeks abroad and in the clouds a thousand things which lie in his own bosom, or before his face. No; during our tour I will add to nothing, except thou command me. All that thou seest shall be the work of men; and thou wilt soon perceive that they do not require the Devil to incite them.

Faustus. And is this all that thou canst afford me?

Devil. I will lead you from step to step; when we have run through this course, another scene will immediately open. Get first acquainted with that which surrounds thee, and then mount upwards. The treasures of the earth are thine; thou mayst command my power: do but dream — do but wish.

Faustus. That is something.

Devil. Only something! Discontented being, thou shalt be able to force Leviathan to further the projects which thou callest good and noble, and the consequences of them shall be thy earnings, and the reward of thy heart.

Faustus. That were more, if the Devil did not say it.

Devil. Who can boast that he has forced the fiend to do good? However, let this thought inflate thy bosom. Faustus, step out of the circle!

Faustus. It is not yet time.

Devil. Dost thou fear me? I repeat, thou shalt spend the moments allotted to thee according to thy own pleasure: yes, Faustus, I will fill for thee the intoxicating cup of enjoyment, as it has never been filled for any other mortal. Thy nerves shall wear away before thou hast emptied it. Count the sands of the shore, and thence thou mayst guess the number of joys that I will strew before thee.

Thereupon he placed a casket of gold near the circle. The figures of the mayoress and a train of lovely maidens then passed by.

Faustus. Ha, devil, who has showed thee the way to my heart?

Devil. Is not my name Leviathan? I have weighed thee, and thy strength. Dost thou respect these?

(He shook upon the ground, from a sack, a quantity of orders of knighthood, bishops' hats, crosses of honour, and diplomas of nobility.)

"No, no; I know Faustus better: knowledge and pleasure are his gods. Remain what you are; these things are vain and futile. Thus, by different bribes may ye all be won; and for the sake of lust or advancement, ye would work bare your hands and your intellects. But, whilst fools toil for them in the sweat of their brow, and in the exhaustion of their mind, do thou enjoy, without care or labour, what I shall serve up. To-morrow, with thy consent, I will conduct thee to the mayoress."

Faustus. But how?

Devil. Accept the conditions, and I will tell thee. Come out of the circle; thou lookest still like a drunken man.

Faustus. I would annihilate myself if it were not for one thought!

Devil. Which is—

Faustus. That I shall only thereby sooner fall into thy power.

Devil. How rash and hasty are men! Learn but to know me, and, if I cannot gratify thy wildest earthly desires, return to poverty, to contempt, and thy starving philosophy. Step forth, I say.

Faustus. The fury of a lion inflames me, and, if hell were to yawn beneath my foot, I would spring beyond the limits of humanity.

He sprang out of the circle, and cried,

"I am thy lord."

Devil. Yes; as long as thy time runs. I lead a mighty man by the hand, and am proud to be his slave.

CHAPTER II.

On the following morning the devil Leviathan
came with all the pomp and retinue of a nobleman
to the inn where Faustus sojourned. He alighted
from his richly caparisoned steed, and asked the
host whether the famous Faustus sojourned there?
The host replied by a reverential bow, and ushered
him into the house. The Devil then advanced to
Faustus, and said to him, in the presence of the
host:

"Your renown, your great talents, and, above
all, your mighty invention, have induced me to
make a wide circuit in my journey in order to
become acquainted with so remarkable a man,
whom the world, in·spite of its lukewarmness,
knows how to value. I came, likewise, to request
your company in the tour of Europe, and shall be
happy to accede to whatever stipulations you may

choose to make, for I am perfectly aware that such a pleasure is above all price."

Faustus played his part agreeably to that of the Devil; and the host hurried out in order to relate the adventure to his household. The rumour was immediately spread, by a thousand channels, through all Frankfort; and the arrival of the distinguished stranger was soon known, from the sentinel at the city-gate to his most worshipful the mayor himself. Away ran the magistrates, as if the Devil drove them, to the senate-house, leaving all the weighty affairs of state to remain unsettled whilst they consulted about this unexpected apparition. The senior alderman, a patrician, who was particularly expert in deciphering the meaning of the signs which occasionally appeared in the political horizon, and had thereby obtained a powerful ascendency in the council, pressed his fat chin into furrows, and his narrow brow into wrinkles, and, with reflection in his little eyes, assured his sapient brethren that " This distinguished stranger was nothing else than a secret envoy of his imperial majesty, who

was come into Germany to observe attentively the
situation, the comparative strength, the disagreements, and the alliances, of the various states and
princes; so that the high and mighty court, at the
opening of the approaching Diet, might know how
to comport itself. And since the imperial court
had always kept a watchful eye upon their re-
public, they must now endeavour to convince this
distinguished visitor of the fiery zeal which they
had always entertained for the high imperial
house, and not let him depart without winning
him over to the interest of the state. That they
must, in so doing, take as their pattern the prudent senate of Venice, who never failed to show
the greatest friendship and honour towards him
whom they intended to deceive."

The subordinate members of the assembly
affirmed that the alderman had spoken like the
Doge of Venice himself; but the mayor, who bore
the alderman a secret grudge, because the latter,
like a true patrician, hated the democratic form of
government, and was accustomed to say, whenever he was outvoted, " Ha, thus it goes when

tradesmen and shopkeepers are made statesmen,"
quickly took up the cudgels against him in these
words:

" Truly laudable and excellent, most sapient
masters, seems to me that which our most prudent
and politic brother has now advanced, were it not
for one single circumstance which unhappily spoils
all. I, indeed, do not make a boast of possessing
the deep visual penetration of the alderman,—a
penetration, my brethren, which can spy out a
storm before it arises ; nevertheless, whether it be
from chance or reflection, I have long foreseen,
and have long foretold, that which is now gather-
ing around us. You must all remember, that at
each of our sittings I advised you not to treat this
Faustus so contemptuously, but to purchase his
Latin Bible for the small sum he demanded.
Even my wife, who is a mere woman, like all
other women, has frequently said that, although
we ourselves neither understood nor could use the
book, we ought nevertheless to have it ; and, on
account of the beautiful letters in the title-page,
and of the curious invention, to make a show of it,

as we do of our golden bull, and attract strangers from all parts. It was likewise fitting that a free and rich state like ours should protect the arts, and give them a helping hand. But I know very well what was in your minds; 'twas envy—sheer envy. You could not brook that my name should be rendered immortal. You could not digest that posterity should read in the chronicle, ' *Sub consulatu* . . . . a Latin Bible was bought from Faustus of Mayence for two hundred gold guilders.' Yes, yes; 'twas that stuck in your gizzards; but, as you have brewed, so may you drink: Faustus is a devilish wild fellow, and a very strange hand to deal with; I saw that proved yesterday. And now that the imperial envoy has travelled hither merely on his account, merely on account of him whom we have treated worse than a poor cobbler, think ye not he will blow us up with the envoy out of revenge, and all our scrapings and grimaces will serve for nothing but to make us appear ridiculous before the citizens? But he who has driven his cart into the mire may draw it out again. I wash my hands of the whole business, and, like Pilate, am innocent of Israel's blindness and destruction."

Here followed a deep silence. The bloody battle of Cannæ, which threatened Rome with ruin, did not terrify her senate more than did this eloquent philippic the enlightened magistracy of Frankfort. Already the mayor triumphed in proud anticipation: he thought even that he had hurled the alderman entirely out of his saddle; when the latter, collecting his political wisdom and heroic strength, hastened to the assistance of the sinking state, and bellowing aloud, *ad majora*, undauntedly proposed "immediately to send an embassy from the council to the hotel, in order to welcome the distinguished guest, and to offer Faustus four hundred gold guilders for his Latin Bible, and thereby to appease him, and to make him favourable to the state."

The mayor scoffed at the idea of giving four hundred gold guilders for a thing which the day before they might, in all probability, have had for one hundred; but his jeers and his scoffs availed nothing. "*Salus populi suprema lex*," cried the

F

alderman; and, with the approbation of the council, he commanded the mayor to entertain Faustus and the envoy in the most sumptuous manner, at the expense of the state.

This circumstance consoled his worship, who willingly displayed his wealth, partly on account of his defeat by the alderman, while the concluding words, " at the expense of the state," put him in good humour. The junior alderman immediately set out with one of the four syndics, and the mayor sent to his house to order every thing proper for the festival. The devil Leviathan was engaged with Faustus in a deep discourse when these ambassadors were announced. They were instantly admitted. They welcomed, with all humility, in the name of the senate, the distinguished guest, and gave him to understand that his noble person, as well as his important errand, were well known to them; assuring him at the same time, in set terms, of their zeal and devotion for the high imperial house. The Devil, upon this, screwed up his features, turned to Faustus, took him by the hand, and assured the speakers that nothing had brought him to their town but the desire of removing from it this great man, whom he had no doubt they knew how to prize. The ambassadors were now somewhat disturbed; however, they soon recollected themselves, and continued thus:

"It rejoiced them highly that they could give him on the spot a convincing proof of the respect which the magistracy entertained for so great a man, as they were authorised to tender to Faustus four hundred gold guilders for his Latin Bible, which they had long been anxious to possess, and preserve as a precious treasure. The illustrious magistracy would also be most happy to enrol him, if it were agreeable, among the number of citizens, and thereby open to him the way to glory and emolument."

This last stroke was added by their own political wisdom; a proof that they, as skilful negotiators, knew how to supply and fill up every vacuum which had been at first overlooked.

Faustus started up in a fury, stamped on the ground, and cried:

"Base, lying, deceitful pack! How long did I not fawn upon you, from the proud patrician down to the shoemaker and the pepper-seller, around whose necks you hang the magisterial insignia, like halters around asses? And did ye not permit me to wait at your dirty thresholds without deigning me a single look? And now that you hear this noble personage sees that in me which you did not, you come and would pay me back in my own coin. But see, here is gold; for which you would barter the Holy Roman Empire, provided you could find fools gross enough to buy the huge, monstrous carcass, without head, sense, or proportion."

The Devil highly enjoyed the rage of Faustus and the downcast looks of the young senators; but they, who had never read Roman history, were not so high-spirited as to fling Faustus a declaration of war from beneath their closely-folded robes of office; on the contrary, they communicated the invitation to the mayor's festival in as unconcerned a tone as if nothing had happened,—a new proof of their expertness in negotiation. Had they, for example, replied to the insult, they would thereby have acknowledged that they felt the force of it; but when they let it fall flat upon the ground, as if it were nothing to any of them, it lost all its power, and assumed the colour of an unfair reproach. Genius alone is capable in such critical moments of like discrimination.

At the word "mayor," Faustus pricked up his ears, and the Devil gave him a significant side-glance. Faustus thereupon took the Bible from the casket, handed it over to the senators, and said, with some degree of complaisance,

"That, upon due consideration, he was determined to make the city a present of his Bible, on condition that they showed the sentence which he marked under, and of which he wrote a German translation on the margin, to the assembled magistrates; and, in remembrance of him, caused it to be written in letters of gold on the wall of the council-chamber."

The senators hastened back to their brethren, as delighted as envoys who, after a ruinous war, return with an advantageous peace. They were received with great joy, and, the Bible being opened at the appointed place, they read—

"And lo! the fools sat in council, and idiots clamoured in the judgment-chamber."

They swallowed this bitter pill, because the presumptive shadow of imperial majesty, in the form of the demon, prevented them from spitting it out. They comforted themselves with having been spared the four hundred gold guilders, and wished each other joy for having escaped so well out of this unpleasant affair. The envoys received a vote of thanks, and it is to be regretted that their names are not handed down to posterity. When at last they spoke of Faustus's well-filled money-chest, the glitter of gold darted like lightning through the souls of all, and each secretly determined to make the man his friend, in order to get possession of it. The alderman shouted, "We must make him a citizen, and give him a seat and voice in the council. Policy demands that we should overstep law and custom, if the advantage of the state depends upon it."

Faustus, in the mean time, strolled out with the Devil; but they found the people of the place modelled after so unsightly a pattern, with such ugly figures and flat features, that the Devil owned he had never seen them equalled, except by the inhabitants of an English town called N—, when dressed in their Sunday's best. "Envy, malice, curiosity, and avarice," said he, "are here and there the sole springs of action; and both places are governed by a pitiful mercantile spirit, which prevents them from being grandly wicked or nobly virtuous. In short, Faustus, there is little to be done in either place by a man of spirit, and we will hurry away from hence as soon as you have brought the mayoress to the point you wish her."

The clock sounded the hour of dinner; the Devil and Faustus, mounted upon noble horses, and attended by a numerous retinue, proceeded to the house of the mayor. They entered the hall of assembly, where all the magistrates awaited them, and, on their appearance, bowed before them even to the dust. The fat, bloated mayor,

after a long speech, introduced them to the wives
of the dignitaries of the corporation, whose figures,
loaded with tawdry ornaments, seemed now to
display a double portion of awkwardness and vul-
garity. They stared like a flock of geese, and
could not satiate themselves with looking at the
dress and physiognomy of Leviathan; but the
mayoress, a native of Saxony, towered above them
all, like an Oriad. The expressive look of Faustus
had attracted her attention, as well as his prepos-
sessing figure, and his fine handsome face. She
blushed when he saluted her, and could find no
other answer to his eloquent address than a few
broken words, which the ears of Faustus caught
like enchanting music. The senators exerted their
wits to the utmost in complimenting their guests,
and all now sat down to the well-spread table.
After dinner the Devil led the mayor by the hand
to a private apartment,—a circumstance which
flattered him extraordinarily, but which was a
dagger-blow to all the other guests, especially to
the alderman.

The mayor, heated with wine, and intoxicated

with the honour which the supposed imperial
envoy showed him, in a bending attitude and
with staring eyes awaited the communication.
The Devil assured him, in soft, silvery tones, how
much he was flattered by the mayor's hospitable
reception, and how very desirous he was to prove
himself thankful; adding, that he carried with
him a number of letters of nobility, signed by the
emperor's own hand, and he would gladly bestow
the first upon him, provided ——

Joy, transport, and astonishment darted
through the mayor's soul; he stood before the
Devil with wide-gaping mouth, and at length
stammered out, "Provided how—what—oh!"
The Devil then murmured softly into his ear:
"His friend Faustus was desperately in love with
the beautiful mayoress, and that for his sake only
he would do it; and if the mayoress would retire
with Faustus for a few moments,—which would
be entirely unobserved amid the noise and confusion of a festival,—he should deliver into her
hand the patent of nobility."

Thereupon the Devil hastened to Faustus, in-

formed him of what had happened, and gave him
the letter of nobility, with certainty of success.
Faustus doubted, and the Devil laughed at his
doubts.

The mayor remained in his cabinet almost
petrified. The sudden glitter of such unexpected
happiness was at once so clouded by an odious
and detestable condition, that he determined upon
rejecting it. But all at once Ambition blew into
his ear: "Ho! ho! Mr. Mayor; to be dubbed
a nobleman at once, and in such an off-hand
manner, as the saying is, and thereby to be placed
on a footing with the proudest of thy foes, and to
raise thy voice in the council like a trumpet, and
appear among those there like a man whom, on
account of his services, his imperial majesty will
exalt above the heads of all!"

Another feeling softly whispered—

"Uh! uh! with my own knowledge and consent to be thus disgraced! But then, again, who
will know it? and what is there in the whole
affair? I receive a certain good in lieu of what
has long ceased to have any charms for me.

The evil consists in the idea alone, and it will be
a secret between me and my wife. But, stating
the case fairly, can I arrive at so high a distinction at a cheaper rate? Will it not be a nail in
the alderman's coffin; and what will the citizens
not say when they see that his imperial majesty
knows how to value me? Shall I not get every
thing into my power, and revenge myself on those
who have thwarted and contradicted me? Ho!
ho! Mr. Mayor; be no fool; seize fortune by the
forelock. Man is only what he appears in the
eyes of the world, and no one asks the nobleman
how he became so. But there is my wife; she
will set herself against my advancement, for I
well know her Saxon prudery."

At that very moment she entered the room,
eager to learn from her husband what the magnificent stranger had confided to him in private.
He looked at her with a roguish leer, but still
with some degree of bashfulness.

Mayor. Well, my chick, suppose I were to
make thee a noblewoman to-day?

Mayoress. Then, duck, the wives of all the

citizens and magistrates would swoon with envy, and the alderman's lady would instantly die of that husky cough which has so long assailed her.

Mayor. That she would, for certain; and I could crush her proud husband beneath my foot. But hark, my chick: it only rests with you to bring all this about.

Mayoress. Who ever heard of wives making their husbands noblemen, duck?

Mayor. Who knows, my child, how many have been made so? But be not terrified; you have driven that cursed Faustus out of his wits. (*The Mayoress blushed; he continued*) Only on his account will the envoy create me a nobleman, and Faustus is to deliver to thee the patent of nobility in private. You understand me, I perceive. Hem! What do you think of the plan?

Mayoress. I was thinking, my treasure, that if these two gentlemen were to change their minds, we should certainly lose the patent.

Mayor. Curse it! so we might. Let us be quick, my mouse; such bargains are not met with every day.

The company had in the mean while dispersed themselves in the garden; and his worship, getting behind Faustus, whispered softly in his ear that "his wife would esteem it an honour to receive the patent of nobility from his hand; and he had only to step up a back staircase, which he would show him, to an apartment where he would find her. That as for himself, he feared nothing from a man who had shown so much honour and conscience." He led him thereupon to the back staircase. Faustus glided up immediately, and entered a chamber, where he found the mayoress: he flew to her, and created the mayor a knight of the Holy Roman Empire. She then went and delivered to her spouse the letter of nobility; and they determined between them that it should be laid upon the supper-table in a covered golden dish, in order, by its unexpected appearance, to make the blow more painful to the guests. The Devil, to whom the mayor confided the plan, highly approved of it; but Faustus murmured in the ear of Leviathan, "I command thee to play this rascal, who has prostituted his wife for am-

bition's sake, a thorough knavish trick; and to
revenge me, at the same time, on all these sheep-
headed magistrates, who so long forced me to pay
my court to them."

　They sat down to supper, and the glasses went
quickly round; when all at once the Devil commanded the dish, which had so long excited the
curiosity of the surrounders, to be uncovered;
then, holding up the letter of nobility, he delivered
it to the mayor with these words: "Worthy sir,
his majesty the emperor, my master, is pleased
by this patent letter of nobility to create you, on
account of your fidelity and services, a knight of
the Holy Roman Empire. I hope and trust that
you will never grow lukewarm in your zeal for
the high imperial house; and now, Sir Knight, I
have the honour of first drinking your health."

These words rolled like thunder in the ears of
the guests. The drunken became sober, and the
sober drunk; the lips of the women turned blue
with rage, and could scarcely stammer out a con-
gratulation. The alderman was seized with an
apoplectic fit, and his wife was near dying of her

husky cough. Fear, in the mean time, obliged
the rest to assume a joyous countenance; and
they drank, with a loud huzza, the health of the
new-made knight. While the tumult was at the
highest pitch, a thin vapour suddenly filled the
hall; the glasses began to dance about upon
the tables; and the roasted geese, turkeys, and
fowls cackled, gobbled, and crowed. The calves,
sheep, and boars' heads cried, bleated, and
grunted, bounced across the table, and snapped at
the fingers of the guests. The wine issued in
blue flames from out the flasks; and the patent of
nobility caught fire, and was burnt to ashes in
the hands of the trembling mayor. The whole
assembly now sat like so many ridiculous characters in a mad masquerade. The mayor bore a
stag's head upon his shoulders; and the rest,
men and women, adorned with grotesque masks,
spoke, cackled, crowed, neighed, or bellowed, according to the kind of mask which had been
allotted to each individual. The alderman alone,
in the dress of a harlequin, sat motionless; and
Faustus avowed to the Devil that the ruse did

great honour to his ingenuity. After Faustus had satiated himself by gazing at the spectacle, he gave the Devil the wink, and they both flew out of the window; the latter personage, according to custom, leaving behind him the sulphurous stench.

By and by the whole illusion disappeared; and when the sapient magistrates re-assembled next morning in the council-chamber, they scarcely mentioned to each other what had taken place the night before. They kept the whole matter a state secret, and only revealed it now and then to a chosen few. All that the mayor got by this business was, that his adversary, the alderman, lost the use of his limbs, and never again took his seat in the council.

Faustus and Leviathan, in the mean time, passed over the city-walls; and when they were in the open field, the Devil despatched an attendant spirit to the hotel, in order to pay the reckoning, and to fetch away Faustus's baggage. Then turning to the young German, he asked him if he were contented with this first feat.

Faustus. Hem! if the Devil wants praise, I am content to give it him. But I should never have imagined that yon pompous scoundrel would have sold his wife for ambition's sake.

Devil. Let us proceed a little further, my Faustus, and I will soon convince thee that Ambition is the godhead which ye all worship; although you disguise it under all kind of glittering forms, in order to conceal its nakedness. Till now you have studied man merely in books and philosophical treatises; or, in other words, you have been thrashing empty straw. But the film will soon fall from your eyes. We will shortly quit this dirty country of yours, where priestcrâft, pedantry, and oppression reign unmolested and undisturbed. I will usher you upon a stage where the passions have a freer scope, and where great energies are employed to great ends.

Faustus. But I will force thee to believe in the moral worth of man before we quit my native land. Not far from hence lives a prince, whom all Germany praises as a paragon of every virtue. Let us seek him, and put him to the test.

Devil. Agreed; such a man would please me for his rarity.

The spirit now returned with the baggage, and was sent forward to Mayence to bespeak a lodging in an hotel. Faustus, for secret reasons which the Devil guessed, proposed spending the night with a hermit who dwelt in the hill of Homburg, and who was renowned through the whole neighbourhood for his piety. They reached the hermitage about midnight, and knocked at the door. The solitary opened it; and Faustus, who had dressed himself in the richest clothes which the Devil had provided for him, begged pardon for disturbing the repose of the holy man, and said that the night had surprised him and his companion while hunting, and had separated them from their attendants, and that they should be obliged by his giving them house-room for a few hours. The hermit looked on the ground, and replied, with a deep sigh:

"He who lives for heaven seldom abandons himself to dangerous repose. You have not disturbed me; and, if you wish to stay here till

sunrise, you must take things as you find them.
Bread and water, with straw to lie on, is all I can
afford you."

Faustus. Brother hermit, we have brought all
that the stomach requires along with us. We
will only trouble you for a draught of water.

(*The hermit took his pitcher and went to a foun-
tain.*)

Faustus. Peace dwells in his heart as well as
on his brow, and I may think myself happy that
he is not. acquainted with that which binds me to
thee. Faith and hope serve him instead of those
things which I have damned myself for; at least
it seems so.

Devil. And only seems. What if I were to
prove that your heart is pure as gold in comparison with his?

Faustus. Devil!

Devil. Faustus, thou wert poor, ill-treated,
and despised; thou didst see thyself in the dust;
but, like an energetic being, thou hast sprung out
of contempt at thy own risk. Thou wert incapable of gratifying thy lusts by the murder of

thy fellow-creatures, as this saint would if I led him into temptation.

Faustus. I see all thy infernal craftiness. If I were to command thee to put him to a fair trial, thou wouldst confuse the senses of the just man, so that he would commit acts which his heart abhorred.

Devil. Ridiculous! Why, then, do ye boast of your free-will, and thereby ascribe your deeds to your own hearts? But ye are all saints while there is nothing to tempt ye. No, Faustus; I will remain neuter, and merely offer delights to his senses; for the Devil has no need to creep into ye when you are already disposed for wickedness.

Faustus. And if things do not turn out as you assert, think not that your assurance shall remain unpunished.

Devil. Thou mayst then torment me a whole day by preaching of the virtues of men. Let us see whether this will allure him.

A table, provided with dainty meats and delicious wines, now appeared in the middle of the hermitage. The solitary entered, and silently

placed the pitcher before Faustus, and then retired into a corner, without heeding the luxurious
banquet.

Faustus. Now, brother hermit, since the things
are on the table, fall to without waiting to be
asked twice. You may eat of our fare without
the least injury to your reputation. I see your
mouth begins to water. Come, a glass to the
honour of your patron saint. What is his name?

Hermit. St. George.

Faustus. Here's his health.

Devil. Ho, ho, brother hermit! the renowned
St. George of Cappadocia was a fellow after my
own heart; and if you take him for a model, you
cannot go wrong. I am perfectly well acquainted
with his history, and will relate it in a few words
for your instruction. He was the son of wretch-
edly poor people, and was born in a miserable
hut in Cilicia. As he grew up, he early perceived
his own talents, and, by force of flattery, servility, and corruption, found his way into the
houses of the great and opulent, who at length,
out of gratitude for his services, procured him a

commission in the army of the Greek emperor.
But when there he pilfered and plundered to so
enormous an extent, that he was soon obliged to
fly, to avoid being hanged. Thereupon he joined
himself to the sect of the Arians, and, by his
quick parts, soon learnt to gabble the unintelli-
gible jargon of theology and metaphysics. About
this time the Arian emperor, Constantine, kicked
from the episcopal chair at Alexandria the good
and most Catholic Athanasius; and your redoubt-
able Cappadocian was, by an Arian synod, appointed to the vacant see. George was now completely in his element: he puffed, strutted, and
filled his paunch. But when he, by his injustice
and cruelty, had driven his subjects to the verge
of madness, they put him to death, and carried
his body in triumph through the streets of Alexandria. Thus did he become a martyr, and consequently a saint.

Hermit. There is not a word of this in the
legend.

Devil. I believe ye, brother; and, for the sake
of truth, the Devil only ought to have written it.

The hermit then crossed himself.

Faustus. Do you call eating and drinking crimes?

Hermit. They may tempt us to commit crimes.

Devil. Your virtue must be very weak if it cannot resist temptation; for temptation and resistance should be the glory of a saint.

Hermit. You are right so far; but every one is not a saint.

Faustus. Are you happy, brother?

Hermit. Solitude makes me happy; a good conscience makes me blessed.

Devil. How do you obtain your food?

Hermit. The peasants bring me wherewithal to support my existence.

Faustus. And what do you give them in return?

Hermit. I pray for them.

Faustus. Are they bettered by your prayers?

Hermit. They think so, and I hope so.

Devil. Brother, you are a rogue.

Hermit. The reproaches of the sinful world are what the just man ought to expect.

Devil. Why do you not look upwards, and
why do you blush? But know, that I have the
art of reading in a man's face what is passing in
his heart.

Hermit. So much the worse for yourself. You
will have little enjoyment in company.

Devil. Ho, ho! you know that? (*Looking at
Faustus.*)

Hermit. It is a vile world in which we live,
and woe for you if thousands did not hasten into
solitude to avert by their prayers the anger of
incensed Heaven from the heads of sinners.

Faustus. Reverend brother, you own yourself
that you are paid for your prayers; and, believe
me, it is much easier to pray than work.

Devil. Listen once more. You have a twist
of the mouth which tells me you are a hypocrite;
and your eyes, which revolve in so narrow a
circle, and which are generally cast downward,
tell me that you are convinced they would betray the feelings of your heart, were you to raise
them.

The hermit lifted his eyes towards the heavens, prayed with clasped hands, and said, " Thus does the righteous man reply to the scoffer."

Faustus. Enough. Come, brother, and bear us company in our repast.

But the hermit remained inflexible. Faustus looked scornfully on the Devil, who merely smiled and shook his head. Suddenly the door opened, and a young female pilgrim rushed in almost breathless. When she had recovered from her fear, she related how she had been pursued by a knight, from whom she had the good fortune to escape by reaching the cell of the pious hermit. She was received in a friendly manner; and, unclasping her long mantle, she exhibited such beauty as would have made the victory over the flesh no easy matter for the holy Anthony himself. She placed herself by the side of Leviathan, ate sparingly of the meal, and the Devil began to—

*　　*　　*　　*　　*　　*

The hermit was at first shocked, and at last confused; and he had scarcely power to struggle with the temptation. The pilgrim tore herself, ashamed and angry, from the arms of Leviathan, to seek protection by the side of the hermit, which he could not refuse her.

The Devil and Faustus now pretended to be intoxicated and overwhelmed with sleep; but before they took repose the Devil placed, in the presence of the hermit, a weighty purse of money under the straw, and deposited his own rich rings and those of Faustus in a casket, which the latter laid close beside him. On the table they placed their swords and daggers, and then flung themselves down and soon snored.

The pilgrim softly approached the table, and poured out with her delicate and snow-white hands a goblet of foaming wine. She just touched the rim with her rosy lips, and then offered it to the hermit. He stood like one amazed; and in his confusion emptied it, and another besides, and greedily swallowed the luxurious morsels which the tempter, one after another, held up to his mouth. She then led him out, and bursting into tears, entreated his pardon for having been forced to outrage his holy eyes. She then looked mournful and inconsolable, pressed his hand warmly, and at last fell down on her knees before him. At this instant the silvery moon beamed upon her bosom, over which the gentle night-wind moved her dark, dishevelled locks. The hermit sank upon this dazzling bosom, without knowing whether he was dead or alive. At length the pilgrim said, "That she would yield herself entirely to his wishes, if he would revenge her first on those daring reprobates, and take possession of their treasure, which would enable him and her to live happily to the end of their days."

The hermit, at these words, recovered in some degree from his intoxication, and asked her, in a trembling voice, what she meant, and what she would have him do.

Amongst broken exclamations of rapture she murmured, "Their daggers lie on the table: do you murder the one; I will manage the other. Then dress yourself in their clothes, and seize their treasure. We will then set the hermitage on fire, and fly to France together."

The horrible idea of murder made the hermit

shudder. He hesitated, was undecided, looked on the charms of the siren; he saw that he could make himself master of her and of the treasure without danger; and, all his virtue yielding, he forgot heaven and his oft-repeated vows. The pilgrim dragged the reeling miscreant into the hut; each seized a dagger; and just as he was about to aim a blow at Faustus, the Devil burst into the fiendish scorn-laugh; and Faustus saw the hermit, with a lifted dagger, standing by his side.

Faustus. Cursed monster, who, under the mask of religion, wouldst murder thy guest!

The hermit sunk trembling to the earth. The pilgrim, a phantom of hell, appeared to him in a frightful form, and then vanished.

Faustus commanded Leviathan to set fire to the hut, and burn it to ashes, along with the hypocrite. The Devil obeyed with joy. The following morning the peasants shed many tears for the fate of the righteous man; and, having collected his bones, they preserved them as precious relics.

Faustus and the Devil arrived early the next day at Mayence, and alighted at the dwelling of the former. His young wife fell with a cry of joy upon his neck, embraced him, and then burst into tears of sorrow. The children clung sobbing to his knees, and greedily examined his pockets, to see whether he had brought them any thing. His old gray-headed father next staggered towards him, and shook him mournfully by the hand. The heart of Faustus was moved, and his eyes began to moisten, while he trembled, and looked angrily upon the Devil. When he asked his wife why she wept, she wrung her hands, and replied, "Ah, Faustus, do you not perceive how the hungry ones examine your pockets for bread? How can I see that without tears? They have eaten nothing for a long time; we have been unfortunate, and all thy friends have forsaken us; but now I see thee again, it is to me as though I saw the countenance of an angel. I and thy father have suffered more on thy account than on our own. We have had such frightful dreams and visions; and when my eyes, weary with

weeping, have closed for a few hours, I saw thee
torn from us by force, and all was dark and
horrible."

Faustus. Thy dream, love, is about to be partly
fulfilled. This gentleman here will reward thy
husband for those talents which his ungrateful
country overlooked or despised. I have agreed to
travel with him far and wide.

Old Faustus. "My son, stay at home and support thyself honourably," says Scripture.

Faustus. And die of hunger, says Experience.

The wife began to weep yet more bitterly, and
the children screamed for bread. Faustus gave
the Devil a sign, and he called to his servant,
who presently afterwards brought into the room
a heavy coffer. Faustus unlocked it, and flung a
large bag of gold upon the table; which being
opened, and the yellow coin appearing, a lively
flush of joy was instantly diffused over the melancholy countenances of the family. He then took
out magnificent clothes and jewels, which he
delivered to his wife. Her tears vanished, and
vanity at once dried them up, as the sun-rays dry

up the morning dew. The Devil smiled, and Faustus muttered to himself, " O magic of gold and of vanity! I may now go to the antipodes, and no other tears than those of hypocrisy will be shed." Then, aloud, " Well, wife, these are the fruits of my journey, reaped in advance. Is not this better than staying at home with you and starving?"

But the wife heard him not; for she stood with her rich robes and jewels before the looking-glass to see how they became her. The little girls frolicked around her, took up the clothes and ornaments she had laid aside, and aped the mother. In the mean time a servant brought in a substantial breakfast, the children fell upon it, cried and shouted with joy; but the mother had, in the mean time, forgotten her hunger.

The old father took Faustus aside, and said, " If thou hast obtained all these things by honourable means, let us thank God, my son, and enjoy his bounty; but for some nights past I have had horrible dreams, although I hope they were merely caused by our necessities."

This remark of the old man sank deep into the heart of Faustus; but the pleasure of seeing his children eat so heartily, and of observing with what love and thankfulness his eldest son and favourite looked at him; the thought of having relieved them from their misery; and, above all, an inward longing for pleasure,—considerably damped the impression. The Devil added a large sum to the money in the bag, presented the young wife with a costly necklace, gave each of the children a trifle, and assured the family that he would bring back Faustus to them safe, sound, and wealthy at no very distant period.

Faustus, attended by the Devil, now went to see a friend, whom he found much dejected. He asked him the cause of his unhappiness, and the other replied:

"This afternoon the law-suit which you have often heard me speak of is to be determined; and I am certain of losing it, although justice is on my side. In short, Master Faustus, nothing remains for me to do but to beg, or drown myself in the deepest part of the Rhine."

Faustus. How can you be certain that you will lose your cause, if justice is for you, as you say it is?

Friend. But the five hundred gold guilders which my opponent has given the Judge are against me; and if I cannot outbid him, I must fall to the ground.

Faustus. Pooh! does it merely depend on that? Come, lead me to the Judge. I have a friend here who willingly assists people out of such difficulties.

They found the Judge to be a proud, inflated man, who would scarcely deign to honour a poor client with a look. Faustus had long known him for what he was. When they entered the room, the Judge, in an imperious tone, thus addressed Faustus's friend, " Why do you come to trouble me? Do you not know that tears never interrupt the course of justice?"

. The unhappy friend looked humbly to the ground.

Faustus. Mighty sir, you have spoken well: tears are like water; they merely spoil the eyes of

H

those that shed them.   But do you know that my
friend has right on his side ?

Judge. Master Faustus, I know you for a man
who plays away his money at ducks-and-drakes,
and who has a loose tongue.   Right and law are
very different things : if he has the first for him,
it is no reason that he should have the second.

Faustus. You say that right and law are two
different things : something like judge and justice,
perhaps.

Judge. Master Faustus, I have already said
that I know you.

Faustus. Perhaps we are mistaken in each
other, most enlightened sir.   But it is mere waste
of soap to attempt to wash a blackamoor white.
(*He opened the door, and in stalked the Devil.*)
Here is a gentleman who will lay before you a
document, which I hope will give the cause of my
friend a new aspect.

When the Judge saw the richly-dressed Leviathan, he assumed a more friendly countenance,
and asked them all to be seated.

Faustus. We can settle the whole business

standing. (*To the Devil*) Produce the document which we have found.

The Devil counted out of his purse five hundred gold guilders; he then stopped and looked at the Judge.

Judge. The document is by no means a bad one, gentlemen; but the adverse party has long ago given me one of equal weight.

The Devil continued counting till he had told out a thousand; he then stopped.

Judge. In truth, I had overlooked this circumstance. Such vouchers, however, are not to be withstood.

He then gathered up the gold and secured it in his coffer.

Faustus. I hope now that right and law will go together.

Judge. Master Faustus, you understand the art of appeasing the bitterest enemies.

Faustus, whom the servility of the Judge as much offended as his former rudeness, whispered to the Devil, in going away, "Do thou avenge justice on this wretch."

Thereupon he left his friend, without waiting for his thanks, and went about with the Devil to discharge his debts. He then paid visits to his other friends, showered gold upon them by handfuls, even on those who had forsaken him in his adversity; and he felt happy in being able to give unbridled scope to his generosity and greatness of soul. The Devil, however, who saw deeper into things than Faustus, laughed within himself at the consequences.

They now went to the hotel. Faustus, recollecting the conduct of his wife, once again fell into an exceedingly ill humour. He could not pardon her for having ceased to lament his departure the moment she had seen the gold and jewels. Till now he had imagined that she loved him more than all the treasures of the earth; but what he had just observed forced him to believe the contrary, and his affection for her was turned to bitterness. The Devil, who perceived where the shoe pinched, willingly allowed Faustus to torment himself with these gloomy thoughts, so that he might tear himself from that sweet tie by which

nature still gently fettered him. He foresaw, with
secret rapture, the dreadful anguish which would
one day arise in the bosom of the headstrong
Faustus, when the future should disclose to him
all the horrors which he was now about to per-
petrate.

They dined in the public room, in company
with some professors of law and divinity, who,
to the great delight of the Devil, soon fell into a
violent dispute concerning the nun Clara. The
flame of that controversy was still at its full
height; party-spirit raged in all houses, and the
present disputants talked so loudly, and said so
many ridiculous things, that Faustus soon forgot
his ill humour. But when a doctor of theology
asserted that it was possible for Satan to have
carried his wickedness so far as to have brought
the nun into certain circumstances by means of
the dream, the Devil burst into a bellowing laugh;
and Faustus immediately thought of a scheme by
which he might revenge himself, in a signal manner, upon the Archbishop, who had paid so little
attention to his discovery. He hoped then to

involve the thread of the theological and political war at Mayence in such confusion that no human power would be able to unravel it. After dinner he asked the demon whether it would be possible for him, under the figure of the Dominican, to pass that night with the lovely Clara. The Devil assured him that nothing was more easy; and, if he chose, the abbess herself should usher him into the nun's cell. Faustus, who had always considered the abbess to be a strict, pious, and conscientious woman, laughed in scorn at these last words of the Devil.

Devil. Thy wife, O Faustus, set up a shriek of despair when thou didst tell her of thy intended departure; but when the glitter of gold and dress burst upon her view, the sorrows of her heart vanished at once. I repeat, that the abbess herself shall introduce thee to the cell of the nun, and I will employ no supernatural means. Thou thyself shalt see how the old gudgeon will swallow the hook. Come, we will pay her a visit under the pious figures of two nuns. I know the manners and ways of the nuns, ay, and of the monks

too, of Germany, well enough to ape them. I
will represent the Abbess of the Black Nuns, and
thou shalt be her friend, Sister Agatha.

At this moment Faustus's friend came, full of
joy, to inform him of the happy issue of the law-
suit. He was about to thank Faustus and the
Devil upon his knees; but Faustus said, " Spare
your thanks, and take care of my wife and family
during my absence." He then whispered into
the ear of the Devil, " It is time to think of the
Judge."

The Judge wished after dinner to gratify his
beloved wife by counting the gold pieces in her
presence. He unlocked the coffer, and started
back in a tremor at the sight of its contents: the
gold pieces were changed into large rats, which
sprang out, and fell furiously upon his face and
hands. The Judge, who had a great aversion to
these animals, rushed out of the room; but they
pursued him, fastening on his heels. He hurried from the house, and ran through the streets;
but still they were close behind him. He fled
into the fields; but they allowed him no rest, and

at last forced the terrified wretch to seek shelter
in the stone tower where the tolls are gathered,
and which stands in the middle of the Rhine.
Here he thought himself safe from further pursuit; but rats and mice hot from hell are not to
be terrified by water: they swam through, fell
upon him, and ate him up alive. His wife, in
her terror and astonishment, told the history of
the transformation of the gold pieces by which
her unfortunate husband had allowed himself to
be dazzled; and from that time there has not
been in the whole diocese of Mayence a single
instance of a judge or a man in office taking a
bribe. The Devil could not have foreseen this,
or he certainly would have let the scoundrel go
unpunished.

Faustus and the Devil stood in their disguises
before the gate of the convent of White Nuns.
The portress ran as fast as she could in order to
inform the abbess of the unexpected visitors. The
abbess received them with conventual greetings,
to which the Devil answered in a similar tone.
Sweetmeats and wines were then brought in, and

while partaking of them the two abbesses talked
together of cloister affairs, and of the wicked
world; and the Devil, with a deep sigh, turned
the discourse to Clara's accident. Clara, who, on
account of her rank, was the pet-lamb of the
cloister, stood near the abbess, and laughed beneath her veil. Faustus observed this, and, looking at her, really thought he had never seen a
more charming rogue wear the sacred veil. The
Devil at length gave the conversation a serious
turn, and led the abbess to conclude that he had
something weighty to confide to her.

Abbess (to Clara). You may go, my lamb, to
the nuns in the garden, and divert yourself with
them; I will send you out some sweetmeats, so
that you may celebrate the coming of our vener-
able sister.

Clara bounded away. After a few words,
which the Devil uttered in a disturbed and
thoughtful kind of tone, so that he might thereby
arouse the curiosity of the abbess, he came to the
point.

Devil. Ah, dear sister, how much do I pity

you! It is true, and that ought in some degree to
comfort you, that the whole city and the entire
district are convinced of your holiness, your piety,
and the strictness of your discipline. In a word,
you possess all the virtues requisite for a bride of
heaven. But, alas, the world will be the world
still; and the Fiend often infuses evil thoughts
into the minds of worldly men, so that through
them he may disturb those saints who are thorns
in his side. No, no; the wicked Devil cannot
bear that you should bring up your lambs in
untainted purity. I pity you, as I said before,
and still more the little innocents who are at present confided to your care. What will become of
them when they lose you?

Abbess. Kind sister, be of good cheer; though
I am old, I am yet, thanks to Heaven, sound and
hearty, and the little inconveniences which attend
a uniform course of devotion and penitence pro-
long life rather than shorten it. So, at least, the
physician of the convent tells me when I complain
to him.

The Devil looked at her attentively.

"Have you, then, had no anticipation of what is hanging over your head? no warning vision? Has nothing occurred in the convent to make you look forward to the future with anxiety? It is customary for pious souls to be informed by certain signs when any disaster menaces them."

Abbess. You frighten me so, that I tremble in my whole body. But let me reflect;—yes, yes, I am very restless, and dream of raw heads and bloody bones; and some days ago—ah, yes!— that certainly was a sign and a warning—some few days ago I went with my lap-dog, which you see there, to walk in the garden. I was alone; the nuns were at some distance, telling stories beneath the linden-trees. All at once the gardener's great mastiff sprung upon *Piety*, for that is the name of my pet. I shuddered from head to foot, and crossed myself again and again; but that would avail nothing. At last I struck at the hideous brute with my staff,—yes, I struck with all my strength the filthy hound who would thus profane the cloister; and I continued striking until the staff, which his reverence the Archbishop delivered to me upon my consecration as abbess, broke in two. Was that a sign or a warning, think ye?

The Devil and Faustus pretended to be shocked.

Devil. Ah, the very worst in the world. All now is but too clear and manifest. Did not I tell you how it would turn out, Sister Agatha?

Faustus made a humble bow of assent.

Abbess. For Heaven's sake, speak, or I shall run mad.

Devil. Contain yourself, dear sister. Help is to be found, and who knows but I bring it with me? Remember that it was the staff which the Archbishop presented to you upon your being consecrated an abbess which you broke; and now listen to me attentively. You know my cousin the prebend; well, he confided to me a very terrible affair. He indeed made me solemnly promise not to tell you; but I know it is best to commit a little sin, if by its means we can prevent a great one and confound the projects of Satan.

Abbess. You are perfectly right; and the

Fathers of the Church hold that doctrine, as my confessor has often told me.

Devil. Know, then, that the Archbishop has so far got the upper hand of the Chapter, that he has brought them to consent to your being deposed after the lapse of a few months, and his niece Clara being made abbess in your stead.

"Jesu Maria!" cried the abbess, wrung her hands, and fell into a swoon. The Devil made a sour face at her exclamation, and Faustus, laughing, rubbed her wrinkled brows. After she had recovered herself, she shed a torrent of tears, and shrieked a thousand curses against the wickedness of the world.

Devil. Do not despair, dear sister. For a distant evil there is always a remedy.

Abbess. And what do you advise me to do? Wretch that I am! O Heavens! what will become of me,—what will become of the nuns?

Devil. I have already said that it is best to commit a slight sin if, by so doing, we prevent a great one, and you yourself have proved it by the authority of holy Fathers; but, dear sister, courage and understanding will be necessary, if you wish to obtain your purpose without danger to your own soul, by loading another person with the capital sin.

Abbess. Ah, dear sister, and how is that to be contrived?

Devil. I was once in our convent in almost a similar perplexity. The good Sister Agatha here is my witness; and as she saw every thing, and assisted me, we may speak out before her.

Faustus bowed with humility.

Devil. A nun who, by sinful wit, and yet more sinful beauty, had found favour among the great and powerful, was, by their assistance, on the point of rising above me. Ah! I have felt how grievous are the thoughts of being forced to obey, after one has for a long time exercised boundless power. Well, in the presence of Sister Agatha, I entered into a consultation with my relation the prebend: he is very knowing in affairs of conscience and crime, and understands to a hair's-breadth what is damnable and what is not. This wise man gave me a piece of advice which helped

me out of my trouble, and for which I shall
always have reason to bless him. I admit that
the expedient at first appeared to me sinful; but
he assured me, and proved to me out of the ca-
suists, that a little fasting and penance would do
away with all that was culpable in it.

Abbess. But the advice—the advice!

Devil. I am ashamed to tell it you aloud.

Abbess. Then whisper it into my ear. What
the Abbess of the Black Nuns could do without en-
dangering her salvation, the Abbess of the White
Nuns may do also.

Devil (softly into her ear). He advised me to
contrive so that this dangerous nun should commit the sin of *   *   *

Abbess (crossing herself). Blessed Ursula!
Why, that is the work of the Devil, and leads
directly to hell.

Devil. Ay, very true, but only the person
who commits it; and I was not advising you to
do it. Remember, dear sister, you are not to be
punished for all the sins which your nuns may
choose to commit.

Abbess. But, in Heaven's name, how did you
manage this dangerous affair without being discovered?

Devil. Oh, my situation was much more difficult than yours, for you are assisted by the report
of the dream, which already fills the whole city.
Suppose, now, you were to let a man, dressed like
the Dominican, slip into Clara's cell, and the signs
of the sinful deed were afterwards to appear,
would not the whole world say that it was a trick
of the arch foe of mankind? Let Satan have the
credit of it, and do you remain sitting in your
chair, adorned with that dignity which Heaven
has been pleased to grant you. I have given you
this advice out of friendship, and for your good;
you are now at liberty to do as you please. At
all events, I will send you some one to-night to
personate the Dominican, and he will only have
to return if you are too scrupulous.

The abbess sat like one amazed, and in her
confusion began to tell her Rosary: "*Ave Maria.*
It is certainly allying oneself to the Devil. Blessed Ursula, illumine my darkness." She cast her

eyes upon the image of the saint. "It would
certainly be a great scandal to the convent. *Ave
Maria*. But then it would be placed to Satan's
account. Perhaps, though, I might be damned
for it. *Pater noster*. And am I now to become a
servant in the cloister, and in my old days to be
tormented by a superior, after I have so long tormented the nuns? This little baggage has already
afforded sufficient scandal to the whole town without this. Alas, when I have no longer authority
to box the nuns about, how will this and that
malignant creature revenge herself upon me! *Ave
Maria*. Well, I have made up my mind, and, for
the good of the cloister, I will continue abbess
the remainder of my days, cost what it will."

The Devil applauded her, and the plan was
soon arranged. Upon going away the Devil said
to Faustus:

"Now, what have I done else than ask the
pride of this old beldame whether it is better to
risk eternal damnation, or to give up that tyrannical power over the poor nuns, which the hand
of Death will soon deprive her of?"

Whatever pleasure Faustus derived from the certainty that his desires would be gratified, he was nevertheless much displeased that the Devil should always be in the right. That same evening the abbess herself introduced him, under the disguise of the Dominican, into Clara's cell while the nuns were at vespers. Clara herself soon appeared, and after she had commended herself to St. Ursula, she laid herself down. Her imagination, which had once been directed to a certain object, often repeated to her in dreams her former vision; and she lay in just such a transport, when Faustus approached her, and embodied the apparition, upon which Clara awoke, and still believed herself merely in a dream. The abbess in the mean time did penance in her cell, and made a vow to fast every week for the good of her soul. But the consequences of this night were horrible to poor Clara.

*　　*　　*　　*　　*　　*

The next morning Faustus took leave of his family. Few tears were shed; but his old father, in a mournful tone, gave him wholesome advice.

As Faustus, with the Devil, rode over the bridge which leads across the Rhine, thinking of last night's adventure, and making comments upon the abbess, he saw afar off a man in the water, who seemed upon the point of drowning, and only feebly struggled against approaching death. He commanded Leviathan to save the man. The Devil answered, with a significant look:

"Think well of what thou requirest; he is a youth, and perhaps it will be better for him and for thee that he ends his life here."

Faustus. Thou fiend, only ready for mischief, wouldst thou have me withstand the sacred feeling of nature? Hasten and save him, I repeat.

Devil. Canst thou not swim thyself? No. Well, the consequences be thy reward; thou wilt repent of this.

He rushed into the stream, and rescued the youth. Faustus consoled himself with the idea of having, by this good act, atoned for the preceding night of sin; and Leviathan laughed at the consolation.

CHAPTER III.

THE Devil now led Faustus through a series of
adventures which were to serve as a prelude to
the most afflicting vicissitudes. What Faustus
had hitherto seen had embittered his heart; but
the scenes which now opened upon him by degrees so wounded his spirit, that his mind was
unable either to support or remedy them; and
only one of the worldly great, or, what is nearly
synonymous, a worker and designer of human
misery, could have witnessed them unmoved.

The Devil and Faustus were riding in close
conversation along the banks of the Fulda, when
they saw beneath an oak-tree a countrywoman
sitting with her children, appearing to be the lifeless image of agony and dumb despair. Faustus,
whom sorrow attracted as much as joy, went
hurriedly up to her, and inquired the cause of her

grief. The woman gazed at him for some time, and it was not until his sympathising look had in some degree melted her frozen heart that she was able, amidst tears and sobbings, to explain herself in the following words:

"In the whole world there are no beings so wretched as myself and these poor children. My husband was indebted to the Prince-Bishop for three years' rent. The first year he could not pay it, on account of the failure of his crops; during the second the Bishop's wild-boars grubbed up all his seed from the ground; and during the third his whole hunting-train galloped over our fields and destroyed our harvest. As my husband had often been threatened by the steward with a distress, he intended to have gone this morning to Frankfort, to sell a fat calf and his last pair of oxen, and with the amount to have paid his rent. But just as he was setting out the Bishop's clerk-of-the-kitchen came, and demanded the calf for his lordship's table. My husband pleaded his poverty, and told him how unjust it would be to take away his calf, which

would fetch a high price at Frankfort. The clerk-
of-the-kitchen answered, that no peasant had a
right to carry any thing out of his master's do-
main. The steward and his bailiffs then came,
and instead of taking my husband's part, he
drove off the oxen; the clerk-of-the-kitchen took
the calf; the bailiffs turned me and my children
out of house and home; and while they were pillaging and carrying off our goods, my husband
went into the barn and cut his throat in despair.
The poor wretch lies under that sheet, and we sit
here to watch the body, so that it may not be
devoured by the wild-beasts, for the priest has
refused to bury it."

She tore away the white sheet which had concealed the body, and fell to the ground. Faustus
started at the horrible sight, while tears gushed
from his eyes, and he cried, "Man, man, is this
thy lot?" Then looking up to heaven, "Oh!
didst thou create this unfortunate man merely
that a servant of thy religion might drive him to
despair and suicide?" He cast the cloth over the
body, flung the woman some gold, and said, "I

will go to the Bishop and tell him your melancholy story. I am certain that he will bury your husband, give you back your goods, and punish the villains."

This circumstance made so strong an impression upon Faustus, that he and the Devil reached the Bishop's castle before he could collect himself. They were received with great civility, and shown into a spacious hall, where his reverence was at table. The Prince-Bishop was a man in his best years, but so enormously corpulent that fat seemed to have overwhelmed his nerves, his heart, and his very soul. He was only animated while eating; all his sense lay in his palate, and he never knew vexation, except when he was disappointed of a dish which he had ordered. His table was so well furnished, that Faustus, whom the Devil had often banqueted by means of his spirits, thought to himself that the Bishop surpassed the master of a thousand arts in his dinners. In the middle of the table stood, amongst other dishes, a large calf's-head,—a favourite morsel with the Bishop. He was engaged, both body and soul, in the feast, and had not yet spoken a single word, when suddenly Faustus exclaimed :

"Gracious sir, do not take it ill of me if I spoil your appetite, but it is impossible for me to look on that calf's-head without telling you of a ·shocking affair which has this day occurred in the neighbourhood of your palace. I hope, from your humanity and Christian mildness, that you will cause those aggrieved to be recompensed, and take care in future that your officers do not again outrage humanity, as they have done in this affair."

The Bishop raised his eyes in wonder, looked at Faustus, and emptied his glass.

Faustus related the story with warmth and feeling; none of those present, however, paid any attention to him, and the Bishop continued eating. Faustus then said: "I think I am speaking to a Bishop, a shepherd of his flock, and am standing among teachers and preachers of religion and Christian charity? My lord, am I right or not?"

The Bishop eyed him scornfully; then calling for the clerk-of-the-kitchen, he said: "What hubbub is this about a peasant who has been fool enough to cut his throat?"

The clerk-of-the-kitchen laughed, told the story as Faustus had done, and added: "I took away his calf because it would grace your lordship's table, and was too good for the Frankfort burghers, to whom he wished to sell it. The steward distrained his goods because he had always been a bad tenant, and for three years had not paid his rent. Thus, my lord, does the case stand; and truly no peasant shall drive any thing good out of your demesne with my consent."

Bishop. Go; you are quite right. (*To Faustus*) What have you now to say? you see that he did his duty in taking the calf; or do you think that the Frankfort citizens ought to eat the fat calves of my land, and I the lean?

Faustus was about to speak.

Bishop. Listen! eat, drink, and be silent. You are the first person that has ever spoken of peasants and such rabble at my table. Verily, if your dress did not declare you to be a gentleman, I should be inclined to think that you were

sprung from beggars, since you speak so warmly
in their favour. Learn that the peasant who does
not pay his rent does just as well in cutting his
throat, as certain people would do in holding their
tongues instead of spoiling my appetite with useless speeches. Clerk-of-the-kitchen, that is a
noble calf's-head.

Clerk-of-the-kitchen. It is the head of Hans
Ruprecht's calf.

Bishop. So, so! Send it me here, and reach
me the pepper. I will cut myself a slice. And
you, Mr. What's-your-name, may as well take a
piece with me.

The clerk-of-the-kitchen placed the pepper-
castor before the Bishop. Faustus whispered into
the ear of the Devil; and at the moment the
Bishop ran his knife into the calf's-head, the Devil
changed it to the head of Hans Ruprecht, which,
wild, horrible, and bloody, now stared the Bishop
in the face. His reverence let fall his knife,
and sank back in a fainting fit; while the whole
company sat in lifeless horror and stupefaction.

Faustus. My Lord Bishop, and ye most reverend gentlemen, learn from this to practise Christian charity as well as to preach it.

He hurried away with the Devil.

The *sang-froid* of the Bishop and his table-companions, and the brutal manner in which he spoke of the fate of the unfortunate suicide, sowed the first seeds of gloomy horror in the breast of Faustus. He revolved in his mind his former experience, as well as what he had seen since he had roamed about with the Devil, and perceived, whichever way he turned, nothing but hard-heartedness, deceit, tyranny, and a willingness to commit crime for the sake of gold, preferment, or luxury. He wished to seek for the cause of all this in man himself; but his own unquiet and doubtful spirit, and his imagination, which always avoided difficulties within its reach, began already in dark dissatisfaction to make the Creator of mankind, if not the author, yet, by his sufferance of all these horrors, at least the accomplice. These impious ideas only required the aid of a few more horrible scenes to derange his understanding entirely; and the Devil inwardly rejoiced in being

able to afford a future opportunity for that purpose. Faustus hoped soon to cure himself of this
sadness at the court of the renowned prince, and
his companion willingly left him in this delusion.
About evening they arrived at a city, at the entrance of which they perceived a crowd of people
assembled round a tower, in which culprits condemned to death were accustomed to pass the last
night of their lives. Faustus, observing that the
people were looking up to the ironed windows
with the deepest sorrow, asked the cause of this
assemblage. Whereupon a hundred voices gave
him an answer.

"Dr. Robertus, our father, the friend of freedom, the protector of the people, the avenger of
the oppressed, sits imprisoned in yonder tower.
The cruel tyrannical Minister, once his friend, has
now condemned him to death; and to-morrow he
is to be executed, because he dared to uphold our
privileges."

These words sunk deep into the soul of Faustus. He conceived a high opinion of a man who,
at the risk of his own life, had dared to stand for-

ward as the avenger of his fellow-creatures. As he himself had just been a witness of the consequences of oppression, he commanded the Devil to carry him to this doctor. The Devil took him aside, and then flew up with him into the tower, and entered the cell of the avenger of the people. Faustus saw before him a man whose daring and gloomy physiognomy was truly disgusting. But the romantic imagination of Faustus pictured, at first sight, the form of a great man, from what he had heard and from what he saw before him. The doctor did not seem much surprised at their sudden appearance. Faustus approached him, and said :

"Doctor Robertus, I come to hear your story from your own mouth; not that I have any doubt, for your appearance confirms all that has been told me of you; I am now convinced that you fall a sacrifice to that tyranny which oppresses the race of man, and which I abhor as much as you do. I come likewise to offer you my assistance, which, contrary to all appearances, can extricate you from this dreadful situation."

The doctor looked coldly upon him, let his face sink into his hands, and replied:

"Yes, I fall a victim to power and tyranny; and, what is most grievous to me, through the means of a false friend, who sacrifices me more to his fear and envy than to his despotic principles. I know not who ye are, and whether ye can save me; but I wish that men of your appearance should know Dr. Robertus, who is to bleed to-morrow in the cause of freedom. From my earliest youth the noble spirit of independence, which man is bound to thank for every thing great that he is capable of, fired my breast; from my early youth the numerous examples of tyranny and oppression which I saw with my eyes, or read of in history, roused my soul and inflamed me to fury. Often did I shed tears because I felt myself unable to avenge the sufferings of mankind. To increase my misery, I read in the history of the Greeks and Romans what advancement man made in virtue when tyrants were put down, and he was left to follow the bent of his own nature. Think not that I am one of those fools

whose idea of freedom is that every one should
do as he pleases. Full well I know that the
capacities of men are different, and that their
situations in life must be different; but when I
considered the laws which should secure to each
individual his life and property, I found nothing
but a wild chaos, which tyrannical power had
artfully mixed up in order to make herself the
sole and arbitrary mistress of the happiness and
the existence of the subject. After this discovery,
the whole human race appeared to me as a flock
of sheep, which a band of robbers had conspired to
plunder and devour by means of laws enacted by
themselves, and to which they themselves are not
amenable: for where is the law that fetters the
rulers of the earth? Is it not madness that those
very people who, by their situations, are most liable to the abuse of their passions, are subservient
to no law, and acknowledge no tribunal which can
call them to account? Misery is near, and promised vengeance is far off; and that chimes-in but
poorly with the feelings and nature of man."

Faustus earnestly listened to all this, looked

furious, and struck his forehead with his hand.
The Devil was quite enraptured with the orator,
who continued:

"The wild indignation which I expressed at
every new act of oppression does honour to my
heart, and therefore I care very little though my
enemies can reproach me for want of prudence;
for what is termed prudence by the world is
nothing else than blind submission, servility, flattery, and being unscrupulous how or in what
manner a place is obtained; but an independent
being like myself seeks for happiness by purer
means. I had the misfortune to be allied, by the
bonds of friendship, to the present Minister from
the time we were at school together. He sought
advancement, and he has the spirit which insures
it; for, from his very infancy, he has endeavoured
to obtain power and riches by principles entirely
opposite to mine; and in proportion as I have
attacked tyrannical forms of government, he has
defended them. We have disputed this delicate
point privately and in public, and my honesty has
always enabled me to defeat him; but as it was

natural that I should have the oppressed part of
mankind on my side, so was it yet more reasonable that he should succeed in winning over all
those who derive advantage from enslaving their
fellow-men. ·As these are the very people who
can open the door of happiness and fortune to
their confederates, so was he soon distinguished and
raised, step by step, to the rank of prime-minister
of the kingdom; whilst I, neglected, despised, and
unknown, remained stationary. The proud despot exerted his utmost to bring me over to his
party by bribery and promise of place; but I saw
that he only wished to make me thereby more
deeply feel his power, and that he felt nothing
more was wanting to complete his triumph than
to have a man of my principles acknowledge him
as patron, and sanctify his arbitrary measures by
coöperating with him. True, therefore, to myself, I the more eagerly exposed and censured the
crimes which he was daily committing. You
must be aware that if he had been capable of
feeling what was great, this hostility would have
inspired him with admiration for a man who took

K

him to task with so much danger to himself; but
it operated in a different manner. The more I
exposed him, the more his hatred against me
increased; and when I, a month ago, published a
paper in which I depicted him in his true colours,
and the people thereupon assembled round his
house, threatened his life, and shouted my name
with enthusiasm, the wretch had the baseness to
send the paper forthwith to the Prince, who had
me tried and condemned to death. Thus the laws
of tyrants condemn me, but the rights of man
acquit me.—I have now told you my history, and
you shall hear nothing more from me. I die
without a murmur, and merely grieve that I
cannot burst the chain which fetters my fellow-
men. If you can assist me, good; but know that
death from the hand of my foe is more welcome
to me than mercy. Leave me now to myself;
return to slavery, while I wing my course to everlasting freedom."

Faustus was confounded at the magnanimity
of the Doctor, and hurried away to reproach the
minister with his injustice, and put him to shame.

The Devil, who saw deeper into matters, perceived that the Doctor was animated with quite a different spirit than that of freedom. The minister gave them an immediate audience; when Faustus spoke to him with much warmth and boldness concerning the situation and opinions of the Doctor. He represented to him how injurious it would be to his reputation to sacrifice a man, whom he once called friend, at the shrine of despotism. He gave him to understand that every man would believe that revenge and fear had actuated him to get rid of so sharp-sighted an observer of his actions. "If your proceedings be just," he continued, "you have, then, nothing to fear from him; if, on the contrary, you are such a man as he declares you to be, his execution will only strengthen his assertion, and every honest man will call you a false friend and an oppressor of your fellow-citizens."

Minister. I do not know you, nor do I ask who you are. The manner in which I bear your reproaches and your epithets will best prove my opinion of you. Consider, now, whether you have

a right to bestow them from mere hearsay, being
yourself unacquainted with the affairs of this
country. I will conclude, however, that you
speak from compassion, and therefore will give
you an answer. I was, and am still, the friend of
Dr. Robertus; and I deplore the necessity which
forces me to deliver up to justice a man whose
talents might have made him useful to his country, had he not perverted them to her destruction. I will not search for the cause of this in his
breast, but will leave it to his own conscience.
For a long time I have tolerated his dangerous
infatuation; but since he has inflamed the minds
of the people for whose welfare I am answerable,
and has placed himself at the head of a rebellion,
he must die, as my own son must, were he guilty
of the like offence. The law has judged him, and
not I; he knew this law, and knew what penalties
rebellion draws down upon its sons. I have nothing to say against the opinion of the people:
when they are no longer misled, I believe they
will consider me as their father. If you please,
you may stay among us; and whenever you can

see any thing really calculated for the people's good, be assured that I shall always pay attention to it.

After these words, which he spoke in a firm and unaltered tone, he retired, and left Faustus, who was unable at the moment to make any reply. Upon going away, the latter said to the Devil, "Which of these two, now, shall I believe?" The Devil shrugged his shoulders; for he generally appeared to be ignorant when concealing the truth would be profitable to himself and injurious to mankind.

Faustus. But why should I ask thee? I will obey the call of my own heart. A man who is so nearly allied to me by his way of thinking shall not die.

If Faustus had been acquainted with some of our modern bawlers for freedom, he would not have been so mistaken in the Doctor; but such a being was a novelty at that period.

The next morning, when the execution was to take place, Faustus went into the grand square, attended by the Devil, and told him in going

along what he was to do. At the very moment
the executioner was about to decapitate the Doctor, who had kneeled down, looking very ghastly,
the latter disappeared. The Devil carried him
through the air beyond the frontiers; and there,
delivering him a large sum of money, he abandoned him joyfully to his fate, for he saw pretty
clearly how he would employ his gold and liberty.
The people raised a wild shout of joy at the disap-
pearance of the Doctor, and believed that Providence had rescued their favourite. Faustus also
shouted, and rejoiced at the glorious action.

Faustus and the Devil now rode to the court
of the Prince of ——.* They soon reached the
court of this prince, who was cried up through all
Germany as a wise and virtuous ruler, whose only
happiness consisted in the welfare of his subjects.

---

* It is not out of fear that I refrain from giving the names
of the German princes who appear in this work, but because,
having discovered the secret springs of their actions, I should
too often have to contradict their lying, flattering, ignorant
historians ; and men who willingly allow themselves to be
deceived, might perhaps doubt the truth of my assertions.
Hercules himself could not clear away all the ordure which
these historians have heaped up.—*Original.*

It is true that the subjects themselves did not always join in this cry; but the prince is not yet born who can give satisfaction to all men.

Faustus and the Devil, by means of their dress and equipage, soon found admittance at court. Faustus regarded the Prince with the eyes of a man whose heart was already prepossessed in his favour; and to carry this prepossession even to conviction, nothing more was necessary than the noble exterior of the Prince himself. He was, or appeared to be, frank and open; endeavoured to please and to win all hearts without appearing to do so; was familiar without laying aside his dignity, and possessed that prudent coldness which inspires respect, though we scarcely know why. All this was blended with so much elegance, urbanity, and decorum, that it would have been difficult for the most acute eye to have distinguished the acquired, the artificial, and the assumed, from the plain and natural. Faustus, who had as yet seen few of those men of the world whose natural characters are swallowed up by political prudence, formed an ideal one out of the

above-mentioned materials; and after he had for
some time visited the court, and believed that he
had obtained a thorough knowledge of the head
personage, the following conversation took place
one evening between him and the Devil:

Faustus. I have hitherto purposely said nothing to you of this Prince; but now, having, as
I flatter myself, caught his character, I venture to
affirm that report is no liar, and I hope to wring
from thee an avowal that he is the man we have
been seeking.

Devil. I guessed, from your beginning, how
you would end. I suppose you verily believe that
you have brought the Devil into a quandary;
but of this anon. Your prince shall be for the
present a thoroughly honest fellow. I will tell
you nothing of the result of the observations I
have made upon him; for, from what I have learnt
at the minister's, there is something going forward which will soon give you ocular demonstra-
tion of his worth; till then keep the idea you have
formed of him in your bosom, and tell me what is
your opinion of Count C., his favourite.

Faustus. Curse it: he is the only person here whom I cannot comprehend. He is the bosom friend of the Prince, and yet is as slippery as an eel, which always escapes through your fingers; and as smooth as a woman is towards her husband when she has resolved to deceive him. But perhaps he is obliged to conceal the emotions of his soul, lest some of those spies who are always hanging round the favourites of princes should take advantage of him.

Devil. His soul! Dost think then, Faustus, that a man who so studiously endeavours to disguise himself has a breast that would bear the light? Never trust him in whom art and subtlety have so far overcome animal nature, that even the signs of his instinct and his sensations are extinguished. When that which works and ferments within you shows itself no more in your face, in your eyes, and in your actions, you are no longer what nature formed you; but are become the most dangerous brutes on the earth.

Faustus. And is the Count such a being as you have described?

Devil. The Count is a man who has travelled much and has made the tour of the courts of Europe, has smoothed down the rugged man, and has sacrificed the noble feelings of his heart at the cold shrine of reason; in short, one of those calculating heads who laugh at your ideal virtue, and act with men like the potters, who dash the work of their hands to pieces if it does not please their fancy. He is one of those who think themselves justified, by their experience, to consider the entire race of men as a pack of wolves who will devour all who put confidence in them. Nothing delights him more than to carry on an intricate state-plot; and he treats a maiden as he does a rose which he plucks from the stalk,—inhales the sweetness, and then very coolly treads it under foot.

Faustus. Malicious devil! and can the man thou hast depicted to me be the bosom friend of the Prince of —— ?

Devil. Time will show what he is to him. I tell thee there is something going forward. Didst thou, by the by, observe the minister this evening?

Faustus. He appeared sad and melancholy.

Devil. He, now, is one of those whom you call honest men. He is just, noble-minded, and attentive to the duties of his situation; but, like all of you, he has a foible to counterbalance his virtues; this is an unbounded tenderness for the other sex: and as he, out of principle, required the blessing of the priest to his pleasures, so did he, after the death of his first wife, make a fool of himself by marrying the woman whom you have seen. Through a few hours' enjoyment he destroyed the fabric of his fortune. She took advantage of his doting fondness, and wasted in luxury, dress, and play, her, his, and his children's property, and involved him in debts to an immense amount. It is true she found in Baron H., whom you know, and who is sole master in the house, a powerful coadjutor. When they were completely aground, and their desires had become more craving in proportion as the difficulty of gratifying them increased, the lady readily agreed to a plan which her minion proposed to her in private, and which was nothing else "than to sell the honour

of her stepdaughter, under an equivocal promise
of marriage, at as high a price as the favourite
would buy it." The minister had not the slightest suspicion of all this; he only felt his lack of
money, the weight of his debts, the full mass of
his folly, and trembled in momentary expectation
of the arrival of his son, whom the wife had driven
from home in order that she might dissipate his
property. The poor youth had in the interval
departed for the Turkish wars, and had been rewarded for his interference with a wooden arm.
I do not say that the favourite might not have
had, at the commencement of this affair, serious
views of marrying the daughter, for he was well
aware of the father's interest with the Prince; but
during these last few days the scene has quite
changed. The Prince has proposed to him an
alliance with one of the richest heiresses in the
land; and he has determined, by one secret stroke,
so entirely to overwhelm the minister and his
whole house, that no one shall dare to cry for
revenge or to complain of him. They will all be
silent, and the minister will be crushed beneath

his foot, like the worm, whose sufferings are un-
heard.

Faustus. But will not the Prince hear of this
deed, and punish it?

Devil. Thine own eyes shall be witnesses of
the issue of the affair.

Faustus. I command thee, under pain of my
displeasure, to play none of thy tricks here.

Devil. Those who by their crimes put the
Devil himself to blush, have very little need of
his assistance. We begin now, O Faustus, to remove the covering from the hearts of men; and
I own that I feel sincere joy in finding that the
Germans are capable of something grand. You,
indeed, are merely the imitators of other nations,
and lose thereby the glory of originality; but in
hell that is not esteemed essential, and good-will
in the cause of wickedness is all that is required.

Faustus passed his time gaily among the women of the court, corrupting all those who were to
be obtained by money or a fine face; whilst the
drama of the favourite was rapidly hastening to
a conclusion. He now revealed his finely-spun

design to Baron H. The latter was to be the instrument of it; and as the glitter of gold was no longer at hand to sharpen his palled passion for the minister's wife, and as the tears of the unfortunate daughter, the misery of the father, and the expected arrival of the crippled son, began to bear heavily upon his tender conscience, he determined at once to free himself of all these burdens. His reward consisted in the Count's undertaking to persuade the Prince to send the Baron on an important mission to the imperial court. In consideration of this, the Baron was to procure the wife of the minister to purloin secretly, from the cabinet of her husband, a certain parchment, considered to be one of the most important title-deeds of the princely house; and which the favourite was well aware would shortly be called for, on account of a certain law-suit with another illustrious family. The Count then hoped to make it appear that the minister, for a sum of money, would have delivered it into the hands of the adversaries, if the favourite's watchfulness had not detected his treachery. The spouse of the minister, who thought that an old man who could no longer supply her with gold for her follies deserved no mercy, readily delivered the paper into the hands of the Baron, for whom she had the most doting fondness.

The minister was walking, in a melancholy manner, up and down his apartment. The sense of approaching shame, and the certainty of deceived love, had removed from him even his daughter, who latterly had been his only consolation. She was weeping in her chamber, and breaking a heart worthy of a better destiny. The minister's meditations were interrupted by his wife, who now came to reproach him, and thereby add to his misery. Baron H. presently entered, and coolly demanded the commission, by virtue of which he was to act at the imperial court. As he brought with him the Prince's order for the same, the minister instantly went into his cabinet to fetch it. In the mean time the lady, who now first heard of the Baron's intended departure, began to rave at him in the agony of despair. No sooner did the minister return with the Baron's commis-

sion than a messenger brought him a note from
the Prince, in which he was commanded instantly
to bring the title-deed into court in order that
it might be laid before the envoy of the adverse
party. The minister searched the cabinet, emptied
all his drawers of their contents, and the cold
sweat of death began to trickle down his face.
He questioned his secretaries and clerks, his wife
also, and his daughter; but to no purpose. At
length he was obliged to resolve, fortified as he
was by his innocence, to expose himself to the
dreadful storm. He hastened to the Prince, who
was sitting alone with the Count, informed him of
his misfortune, assured him of his innocence, and
submitted to his destiny. The Count allowed the
Prince to give way to his first indignation at this
unwelcome intelligence, when, advancing very
coolly, he took the title-deed out of his own
pocket, and delivered it to the Prince with a low
bow. He then suffered himself to be closely
questioned as to the means by which the deed
came into his possession; but not until the Prince
had threatened him with his displeasure did he

confess, with the greatest apparent reluctance, the process of the affair according to his concerted plan. The minister was dumb; this evidence of his guilt so confused him, that not even the consciousness of his innocence could dispel the darkness which had come over him. The Prince looked furiously upon him, and said: "I ought long since to have expected that you would endeavour to pay the debts of your waste and extravagance by betraying me." This last reproach in some degree restored the wretched man to his senses; he was about to speak, but the Prince commanded him to be silent, to resign his situation immediately, go home, and not leave his house till sentence should have been pronounced upon him.

The minister accordingly went home, while big tears rolled down his cheeks. Despair forced from the daughter the secret of her shame, and from the wife the avowal of her crime. The strength of his spirit gave way, his senses became confused, and that most frightful of all visitations, insanity, drew a gloomy veil over the remembrance of the past, and, by the ruin of his mind,

healed his heart of the wounds which his nearest
and dearest had inflicted upon it.

It was at this moment that the Devil led
Faustus into the chamber of the minister, having
previously informed him of every particular of the
affair. All the fibres of feeling were not yet entirely destroyed, and some few drops of paternal
sensibility were yet falling from the eyes of the
good old man upon the miserable daughter who
was clasping his knees. He smiled once more,
played with her dishevelled locks, and smiled yet
again. Suddenly his son rushed in, and was
about to precipitate himself into his embrace.
The father gave him a ghastly look; a wild
shriek of madness, which thrilled through the
nerves of every one present, burst from his heav-
ing breast; and the poor sufferer became for ever
an object of horror and painful compassion.

Faustus raged, and uttered the most frightful
curses. He instantly determined to inform the
Prince of the whole proceeding, and to unmask
the traitors. The Devil smiled, and advised him to
go softly to work if he wished thoroughly to know

this Prince whom he boasted of as an imperson-
ation of all human virtues. Faustus hastened to
court; and certain, as he imagined, of being able
to cause the ruin of the favourite by this discovery,
he coolly communicated every thing to the Prince.
When he came to the motive which urged the
Count to this horrible action, namely, his wish to
free himself from his engagements with the daughter of the minister, the countenance of the Prince
brightened; he sent for the Count, and embracing
him on his entrance, said:

"Happy is the Prince who finds a friend who,
out of obedience and the fear of displeasing him,
dares commit an action which the common rules
of morality condemn. The minister has always
acted like a fool. I am glad that we have thus
got rid of him. Thou wilt fill his situation much
better."

Faustus stood for a moment petrified with
horror. Noble warmth soon, however, began to
fire his breast. He depicted in frightful colours
the present situation of the minister. He then
burst into fury and reproaches, and, without the

least reserve or fear, spoke like an avenger of humanity when unmasking a cold-blooded, hypocritical tyrant. He was turned out of the palace as a madman. He returned home, and the Devil received him with a triumphant air. Faustus said nothing, but gnashed his teeth, and, in his venomous wrath, rejoiced that he was entirely separated from the race of man.

About midnight the Count caused the Devil and Faustus to be arrested, and cast into a frightful dungeon. Faustus commanded the fiend to submit quietly, because he wished to see how far these hypocrites would carry their wickedness. When in prison, the dreadful scene of the day flitted before his mind's eye in colours of tenfold horror; and wild thoughts against Him who rules the destiny of man arose from the contemplation of it. His soul became inflamed; and at length he exclaimed, with scornful laughter:

"Where is here the finger of the Godhead, and where is that Providence which presides over the path of the righteous? I see the just man insane, and the wretch who drove him to madness

rewarded; I disclosed to the tyrant, who affects
virtue, the wickedness of his favourite, and he
found him only so much the more worthy of his
friendship and favour. If this be the order and
harmony of the moral world, then there is harmony and order in the brain of the poor lunatic,
who is suffered to fall unprotected and unre-
venged."

He continued, while the Devil listened and
laughed: "But allowing that man is obliged,
by necessity, to do every thing he does, then must
his deeds and his actions be ascribed to the Supreme Being, and they thereby cease to be pun-
ishable. If nothing but what is good and perfect
can flow from a Perfect Being, then are our deeds,
horrible as they seem to us, good and perfect. If
they are wicked, and in reality what they seem
to us, then ought that Being to be looked up to
with horror and aversion. Come, fiend, resolve
my doubts, and tell me what causes the moral
misery of man."

Devil. A truce to your doubts! no one clothed
in flesh is permitted to untie that knot, and *there-*

fore a thousand fools will hang, drown, and destroy themselves. Do not, O Faustus, forget the end which we proposed to ourselves at our first interview. I promised to show thee men in their nakedness, in order to cure thee of the prejudices thou hadst imbibed from thy books, so that they might not disturb thee in the enjoyment of life. But when thou hast rid thyself of all these human frailties, and hast discovered that the pretended guidance of the Eternal One whom thou hast renounced on my account, and before whose sight thou mayst commit, undeterred, the most horrible atrocities, is only a delusion, perhaps thy soul will then have sufficient strength to understand these horrible mysteries; and, if so, I will reveal them to thee.

Faustus. Then, by the mysteries of evil which surround men from their birth to their grave, I shall yet be the greatest of my race; for, in summoning thee, I shall have threaded the labyrinth in which the rest must grope about to all eternity.

Devil. It is well that the rest of men do not

possess the magic art which has enabled thee to render me thy subject, else would hell soon be emptied; and thou wouldst see more devils walking upon the earth than there are saints in the Calendar. Heigh ho! I know what a troublesome life a devil has who is forced to put in execution all the designs of an honest heart and a sound head: what, then, would become of us, if every rascal and fool could call us out of hell!

This observation of the Devil's was on the point of putting Faustus into a better humour; but his attention was almost immediately directed to another subject. Six armed men, with dark lanterns, followed by two executioners with empty sacks, now entered the dungeon. Faustus asked them what they wanted; and the leader answered, with great politeness: "We are merely come, sir, to request you and your honourable companion to creep into these sacks; for we are ordered to tie you up in them, and then fling you into the neighbouring stream." The Devil laughed aloud, and exclaimed: "See, Faustus, the Prince of —— wishes to cool in you that enthusiasm for virtue which you displayed so warmly before him to-day." Faustus looked furiously, and gave a sign: a fiendish roar instantly filled the arched vaults; the soldiers and executioners sunk trembling to the ground, and out flew the prisoners on the wings of the mighty wind.

Revenge now inflamed the breast of Faustus, and arrayed itself in the brilliant hues of a great and noble call. The idea of avenging mankind on its oppressors rushed through his brain, and he determined to employ the power of the Devil in clearing the earth of hypocrites and villains. He therefore exclaimed:

"Fly this moment to the palace, and strangle the wretch who makes a game of virtue. Annihilate him who rewards the traitor, and knowingly treads upon the righteous man. Avenge mankind on him, in my name."

Devil. Faustus, thou art forestalling the vengeance of the Avenger.

Faustus. His vengeance sleeps, and the righteous man suffers; I will have him destroyed who wears only the mask of virtue.

Devil. Bid me, then, breathe pestilence and
death over the whole earth, so that the whole race
of man may perish. I tell thee, Faustus, thou
art giving thyself useless trouble, and sending
wretches down to hell in vain; for things will still
go on as they did, or perhaps worse.

Faustus. Crafty fiend, thou wouldst willingly
save him in order that he might commit more
crimes. Princes like him do indeed deserve thy
protection, for they render virtue contemptible by
rewarding villany. Die he shall, and, loaded with
his last deed, sink trembling into damnation.

Devil. Know, thou fool, that the Devil rejoices
over the death of a sinner; and what I said was
merely to secure myself from thy future reproaches, and that thou mightest have no excuse
remaining. The consequences of this deed be
thine.

Faustus. Yes, be they mine. I will lay them
in the scale against my sins. Hasten, and be firm.
Be thou the arrow of my vengeance. Seize the
favourite and hurl him among the sands of burning Libya, so that he may perish by inches.

Devil. Only private revenge, and spite in finding thyself deceived, drive thee to this.

Faustus. Babbling fiend! It is a solitary remnant of what you call my youthful prejudices which inspires me with angry thoughts at the sight of any atrocious act. If I could have seen and tolerated the wickedness of men, should I have wanted thee? Hasten and obey.

The Devil suffocated the Prince on his magnificent couch, then seized the trembling favourite and hurled him among the burning sands of Libya. He then returned to Faustus, and cried, "The deed is done!" They once more mounted the rapid winds, and sailed out of the country.

Faustus sat, melancholy, upon his horse; for, after they had passed the frontiers, the Devil had changed their method of travelling. The history of the minister still gnawed his heart, and he was stung to the quick at being obliged to acknowledge that the Devil had as yet been right in respect to men; and the bitterness of his spirit increased in proportion as they displayed themselves to him in their true colours. Yet the idea

of having avenged the unfortunate minister upon
the hypocrites cheered him in the midst of his
gloomy sorrows. Pride by degrees so inflated his
heart, that he almost began to consider his alliance
with the Devil as the act of a man who yields up
his soul for the good of his race, and thereby sur-
passes all the heroes of antiquity, who merely
sacrificed their temporal existence; nay more, for
as they sacrificed themselves for the sake of glory,
or for a recompense,—which he, on account of his
engagement, could entertain no hopes of,—so at
last he imagined that they were not worthy to
stand for a moment in comparison with him.
Thus, place men in whatever situation you will,
they soon begin to feel happy, provided their self-
love has an opportunity of working; for self-
love can even gild the yawning gulf of hell, as
in the case of Faustus. He forgot, in his pride,
the motives of his alliance with the Devil, and his
thirst for pleasure and enjoyment; and while he
sat upon his horse, his imagination dubbed him
the knight-errant of virtue and the champion of
innocence. The Devil rode by his side without

once disturbing his meditations; for he only saw in each of these would-be noble feelings the sources of future torment and despair. His hatred of Faustus, however, increased in proportion as the ideal prospects of the latter brightened and expanded; he enjoyed, in anticipation, the hour when all these airy visions would melt and disappear, and all these painted images of fancy would deck themselves in the livery of hell, and tear the rash one's heart as the heart of mortal had never yet been torn. After a long silence, Faustus suddenly exclaimed: "Tell me how it fares with the false favourite."

Devil. He pants upon the scorched sands, and stretches his parched tongue from out his burning jaws, that the air and dew may refresh and moisten it; but no cooling wind blows there, and for a millennium there will fall no refreshing drop from heaven. His blood boils like molten metal in his veins, and the rays of the sun fall perpendicularly upon his bare head. Already is a curse against the Almighty conceived in his inflamed brain, but his tongue is unable to stammer it forth. He turns up the hot sand like a mole, in order that he may suck the damp earth; but thus he only digs his own grave. Is thy revenge satisfied?

Faustus. Revenge! Why dost thou call the exercise of justice revenge? Here am I shedding cold drops of sweat through my skin at what thou hast been telling me; but I saw him laugh when I described to him and his patron the sufferings of the noble father and the ruined daughter.

Devil. Time, which slowly draws up the curtain, will at length disclose every thing. If the villanies of a petty despot and his catamite horrify thee, what wilt thou think when thou seest men who have a thousand times more power, and consequently will, to commit evil? We have, as yet, only removed the first skin of the monster: what will become of thee when we tear open his breast? Soon would He, to whom vengeance properly belongs, empty the magazine of his thunder, were he to destroy all those who, according to thy opinion, do not deserve to live.

Faustus was about to reply, when he saw afar

off a village in a blaze. As every thing uncom-
mon excited his curiosity, he spurred forward his
horse, and the Devil followed at his heels. He
was soon met by a confused rout of knights and
attendants, who had been vanquished by another
party, which, however, did not pursue them.
When they came nearer to the village, they found
the plain strewed with the bodies of men and
horses. They saw among the dead a miserable
wretch, who, with both his hands, was endeavouring to force back his entrails, which were hanging
out of his mangled belly. He howled and cursed
frightfully during this horrid operation. Faustus
asked him the cause of all this bloodshed. The
fellow screamed, " Get to the Devil, Mr. Curiosity;
if you saw your inside outmost, as I see mine, you
would have no wish to answer questions. If you
want to know why they have served me thus,
inquire of that noble gentleman, my master, who
lies there dead, and whom I have to thank for
this treatment."

They left him, and approached a knight who
was wounded in the shoulder, and Faustus put

the same question to him. The knight answered:
" A boor belonging to yon burning village killed,
some time ago, a stag, the property of the mighty
Wildgrave. Thereupon the Wildgrave demanded
the culprit of my master, in order that he might
be tied upon the back of a stag and run to death,
according to the German custom. My master
refused to give up the boor; but in order to punish him, seized every thing he possessed, and confiscated it to his own use. The Wildgrave then
sent a letter of defiance to my lord, in the name of
Heaven, and with the permission of the emperor.
We were worsted in the battle, and the Wildgrave has set fire to the village, which he has surrounded with his horsemen, so that the inhabitants cannot escape; for he intends to fulfil the
oath which he swore, viz. to roast all the peasants,
like Michaelmas geese, for his hounds and wild-
boars."

Faustus (*furiously*). Where is his castle?

Knight. On yonder eminence; it is the strong-
est and most magnificent castle in the whole
country.

Faustus rode to the top of a hill, and looked down upon the burning village, which lay beneath him in the valley. Mothers with children in their arms, old men, youths, and maidens rushed out, cast themselves at the feet of the horsemen, and begged for mercy. The Wildgrave shouted till the valley reëchoed, "Drive the rabble back; they shall perish in the flames!" The peasants screamed out, again and again: "We are innocent! we are innocent! He who offended you has escaped. What have we and our children done? Ah, spare but them!" The horsemen whipped them up from the ground, and drove them into the fire. The poor mothers flung down their babes, in the hope that they would pity them; but the hoofs of the horses trampled them to death.

Faustus cried deliriously: "Fly, Devil, and return not till thou hast consumed the tyrant's castle, and all that is therein. When he returns home, let him find retribution."

The Devil laughed, shook his head, and flew away; whilst Faustus flung himself down beneath a tree, and gazed impatiently upon the castle.

When he beheld it in flames, the madman imagined that he had restored all things to their right order, and received the Devil on his return with the utmost joy. The latter came back in triumph, and boasted of the ruin he had caused; and, pointing to the Wildgrave and his myrmidon, who were scampering towards the castle, he exclaimed: " The vapours of the hellish pool will not, one day, strike him with such horror, O Faustus, as this thy deed: his young and beloved wife was a few days ago delivered of her first-born."

Faustus. Oh, save her and the new-born babe!

Devil. It is too late. The mother pressed the boy in her arms, and he was burnt to ashes upon her bosom.

This episode made Faustus shudder, and he exclaimed, " How ready is the Devil to destroy!"

Devil. Not so ready as daring men are to decide and punish. Had ye but our might, ye would long ago have shattered the vast globe, and reduced it to a chaos. Are you not a proof of this yourself, since you so madly abuse the power

which you have over me? Go to; go to. The
man who does not bridle himself resembles the
wheel which rolls down the steep: who can stop
its course? It springs from rock to rock till it is
shivered. Faustus, I would willingly have permitted the babe to grow up and commit sin; for
I am now deprived both of him and his mother.
Yes, Faustus; she endeavoured to preserve him
from the scorching flames with her arms, the flesh
of which was already frightfully burnt.

Faustus. Thou drivest it home to my very
heart. (*Hiding his face in his mantle, already wet
with his tears.*)

The desire of avenging the virtuous and the
innocent upon the wicked now began to cool in
the heart of Faustus. He however comforted his
spirit, tormented by the last spectacle, with the
thought of the mother and the suckling being
preserved from hell. Besides this, his hot blood,
his eagerness for pleasure, his desire for change,
and finally his doubts, did not permit any sensation to make a lasting impression upon his heart.
As he was attracted by every new object, his feel-

ings, therefore, burnt like sky-rockets, which for
a moment illumine the darkness of the night, and
then suddenly disappear. The rich meal and the
delicious wines which he enjoyed in the next city
where they arrived soon chased away his melancholy fancies; and as the grand fair was being
held there at that time, Faustus and the Devil,
after they had dined, went into the market-place
to see the crowd.

They now found themselves in a strange city.
There lived in one of the convents a young monk,
who had, by means of a heated imagination, succeeded in so powerfully convincing himself of the
force of religious faith, that he believed he should
be able to remove mountains, and to prove himself
a new apostle in deeds and miracles, if once his
soul received the true inspiration, and the Holy
Spirit worked its way through him. Besides this,
he imbibed all the follies and quackeries which
others had rejected,—a circumstance in which
visionaries entirely differ from philosophers. The
young monk, like every theorist who is inspired
with the importance of his subject, was a fiery

orator; he thereby soon won over the minds of
the simple, especially of the women, who were
easily caught by any warm and impassioned ap-
peal. His imagination, however, quickly formed
for him another magic wand; for as he, on account
of his alliance with the highest of all beings, had
a lofty opinion of man, he formed the design of
physiognomically dissecting the masterpiece of
creation, this favourite of heaven, and of allotting
to him his interior qualities by means of his exterior appearance. Men of his character so frequently deceive themselves, that it is impossible
to say whether some remaining spark of understanding had whispered to him that this new
delusion would give a fresh polish to the old one;
and that more pious souls would come to him
than ever, in order to be told so many wondrous
things about their faces. As he had only seen
the four walls of his cell, his penitents, and people
of his own cast, and as he was as ignorant in regard to mankind, the world, and true science, as
men of sanguine imaginations usually are,—it may
be concluded that fancy alone excited him· to this

scheme. His words and his writings operated prodigiously upon the minds of all those who would much rather be confused than think clearly. This is the case with the greater part of mankind; and, as the hours of life glide away very pleasantly when self-love is tickled, it was impossible that he should be without disciples, for he flattered every body. Our monk did not confine his researches to man alone; for he descended to the more ignoble beasts of the earth, allotted to them their qualities by examining their faces and the structure of their bodies, and imagined that he had made a wonderful discovery when he proved —from the mighty claws, the teeth, and the aspect of the lion, and from the tender, light fabric of the hare—why the lion was not a hare, and the hare a lion. He was strangely surprised that he had succeeded in pointing out so clearly the appropriate and unalterable signs of brute nature, and to be able to apply them to man,—although society has so much accustomed the latter to mask his features, that they are rarely to be seen in their primitive state. Not satisfied with these triumphs,

our monk descended even into the kingdoms of
the dead—tore skulls from the graves, and the
bones of animals from the muck-heaps; and
showed his visitors why the dead were dead, and,
from their bones, how it was impossible that they
should be otherwise than dead. In a word, he
proved, clearly and unanswerably, that death
never yet came without a cause.

The Devil was well aware of the general infatuation, and perceived that, while he and Faustus
sat at dinner in the public room, some of the company, and even the innkeeper himself, were sur-
veying them with the utmost attention; and were
communicating to each other, in whispers, the result of their observations, and showing the profiles
which they had secretly taken. The fame of the
wonderful monk had long since reached the ears
of Faustus; but he had hitherto paid so little attention to it, that he now hardly knew what to
make of these signs and whisperings. When they
arrived in the market-place, they were surprised
by a new and extraordinary spectacle. This re-
sort was the true school for physiognomists. Every

one there could single out his man, lay his visage
upon the balance, and weigh out the powers of
his mind. Some stood gazing at horses, asses,
goats, swine, dogs, and sheep. Others held between
their fingers spiders, butterflies, grasshoppers, and
other insects, and endeavoured to ascertain what
their instinct might be from an attentive survey
of their exterior. Some were employed in judg-
ing, from the weight of jaw-bones or the sharpness of teeth, to what animals they belonged.
But when Faustus and the Devil advanced among
them, each man desisted from his occupation, and
began to cry out, "What a nose! what eyes! what
a searching glance! what a soft and beautiful
curve of the chin! what strength! what intuition!
what penetration! what a cleanly-made figure!
what a vigorous and majestic gait! what strength of
limb! how uniform and harmonious is his whole
frame!" "I would give I know not what for the
autographs of the gentlemen," said a weaver, "in
order that I might judge, by their handwriting,
of the quickness of their thoughts." The Devil
happening to knit his brows from impatience of

this folly, one of the physiognomists instantly said, "The internal force of the lion, which the gentleman possesses, has been aroused by some external provocation, or some trifling thought."

Faustus was laughing at all this, when suddenly a beautiful female looked down upon him from a window, and cried, in sweet amazement: "Holy Catherine! what a noble head! what soft and angelic pensiveness in the eyes! what a sweet and lovely physiognomy!" These melodious words sunk into the heart of Faustus. He looked up to the window: her eyes met his for a moment ere she drew herself back. Faustus whispered to the Devil: "I will not quit this town till I have possessed that maiden: what voluptuousness beams in her eyes!" They had scarcely entered a side street, when one of the physiognomists came up and asked them very civilly for "the physiognomy of their writing," assuring them that no stranger had hitherto refused him this favour, and he hoped and trusted that they would not. He thereupon pulled out his album, and offered it to Faustus, at the same time producing pen and ink.

Faustus. Not so fast, my friend; one good turn deserves another. Tell me, first, who the maiden is that I this moment saw at the window of yonder house, and whose countenance is so celestial.

Physiognomist. Ah! she is an angel in every sense of the word. Our illustrious master has often assured us, that her eyes are the very mirrors of chastity, her lovely mouth only formed to express the inspiration of a heart filled with heavenly ideas; that her brow is the polished shield of virtue, against which all temptations, all earthly sin, will be shivered; that her nose snuffs the odours of the fields of bliss; and that she is the most perfect cast of ideal beauty ever yet permitted to appear in the world.

Faustus. Truly, you have depicted her to me with more than earthly colours; and now tell me her situation in life, and her name.

Physiognomist. She is the daughter of a physician; but her father and mother being lately dead, she lives by herself on her own property. Her name is Angelica.

They then wrote some nonsensical lines in his album, and the physiognomist departed, delighted with his treasure.

Faustus. Now tell me, Devil, how this child of grace is to be come at. I am just inclined to see this monk's ideal beauty.

Devil. By the high road to the human heart you will certainly meet her; for sooner or later all must fall in with it, however far their fancies may have caused them to stray from it.

Faustus. What a delightful enjoyment it would be to fill so exalted an imagination as hers with images of pleasure !

Devil. The monk has already had the start of you, and has so sharpened her feelings, and filled her little soul with so much vanity and self-conceit, and made her piety so carnal, that you have nothing else to do than give one audible tap at the gate of her heart, in order to be admitted. Let us now see to what lengths such delusions will lead a young woman.

Faustus. And let it be done quickly.

The Devil was perfectly willing to steal so

pure a soul from heaven, and thereby to consummate more speedily the measure of Faustus's sins. He suddenly stood in the shape of an old man with a peep-show, and, giving Faustus the wink, he hurried away into the market-place. He raised his voice, and invited the people to come and see his peep-show. The populace flocked around him,—footmen and chambermaids, wives and widows, boys and graybeards. The Devil showed them all kinds of scenes, which he accompanied with pious explanations and moral sayings. Each person stepped back delighted from the peep-show, and charmed the bystanders with the recital of the wonders he had witnessed. The beautiful Angelica now looked out of her window; and, hearing the Devil descant in so pious a tone, she felt an irresistible desire to see the wonders of his box, and to bestow alms upon the devout old showman. The Devil was sent for. Even he was struck by her wondrous beauty, her gentle manners, and her ingenuousness; but he became only so much the more desirous to confuse her senses and entrap her. She placed her enthusi-

astic eye to the window of the box. The Devil
preluded with a few proverbs and wise saws, and
unfolded to her view scenes of love, in which he
led her fancy so adroitly from the spiritual to the
carnal, that she was scarcely aware of the grada-
tion. If she were about to turn away her eyes
with shame, the offensive object changed itself at
once into a sublime image, which again attracted
her attention. Her cheeks glowed, and she believed herself gazing upon an unknown and
enchanted world. The artful Devil caused the
figure of Faustus to appear in all these scenes.
She saw him pursuing a shadow which resembled
her own, and undertaking for its sake the greatest
actions, and exposing himself to dangers of every
description. When the Devil had completely
chained her attention, and perceived that she was
highly curious to know wherefore the figure of
Faustus was thus associated with her own, he
changed the scene, and represented the parties in
situations not to be misconstrued. Lightning
does not so quickly glance through the darkness
as did these scenes flit before the eyes of the in-

nocent maiden; a moment is an age in comparison, and the poison was glowing in her breast before she was able to retreat. She started back, and, with her hands before her eyes, rushed into her chamber, and sunk senseless into the arms of Faustus. When she became aware of her fall, she hid her face and repulsed the miscreant. He laid costly jewels at her feet; but she spurned them, and cried, "Tremble, thou wretch! the hand of the Avenger will one day fall heavily upon thee for this crime."

The insensate Faustus rejoiced at his victory; and went, without the least feeling of repentance, to the Devil, who laughed at the affair, and yet more fiendishly when he thought of its terrific consequences.

Faustus found himself here in his element. He flew from conquest to conquest, and made very little use of the power of the Devil, but a great deal of his gold, which has some influence even over devout minds. Angelica became invisible, and all the endeavours of Faustus to see her once more were of no avail; but he soon forgot her in the tumult of his pleasures. Reading by chance some of the manuscript publications of the monk, he was irritated by the self-conceit and ignorance of the author. He proposed to the Devil to play him a trick, and with that intention they both went to the convent. As they were exceedingly well dressed, and appeared to be persons of distinction, they were received by the young monk in the most cordial and friendly manner. His eyes had scarcely met those of the Devil when he became so agitated by his physiognomy, that, forgetting all the forms of politeness, he shook him violently by the hand; and going to some distance, he looked at him first full in the face, and then in the profile. He then cried out:

"Ha! who art thou, most mighty one? Yes; you can do what you like; and what you wish you can also do: your physiognomy tells me this; therefore it is not necessary for me to know you. Never have I been more perfectly convinced of the truth of my science than at this moment. Who can behold such a human visage without

interest, without admiration? Who cannot perceive in that nose, original greatness; in that eye,
penetration, strength, and expression?"

He felt his forehead, and then continued:

"Permit me, with my measure, to ascertain
the height of your brow? Yes; I see unshaken
courage in that forehead, as clearly as I do stead-
fast friendship, fidelity, love of God and man, in
those lips. What a nobleness in the whole! Thy
face is the physiognomy of an extraordinary man,
who thinks deeply, who holds fast to whatever he
undertakes, works, flies, triumphs, finds few men
in whom he will confide, but many who will rely
on him.

"Ah! if a common mortal had such a brow,
such a mouth, such a nose, or even such hair,
what would become of physiognomy?

"Perhaps there is not a man existing whom
thy countenance would not by turns attract and
repel. What infantine simplicity! What heroic
grandeur! Few mortals can be so well known
and so little known as yourself.

"Eagle, lion, destroyer, reformer of mankind,

move on, move on, and reclaim men from their blindness; share with them the intellectual strength which nature has given thee; and announce thyself to all as I have just announced thee to thyself."

Faustus craunched his teeth while the monk was saying all these noble things about the countenance of the Devil, who turning coolly to the physiognomist, said,

"And what is thy opinion of that gentleman? Tell me what he is."

Monk. Great, bold, mighty, powerful, soft, and mild; but thou, his companion, art greater, bolder, mightier, more powerful, more soft, more mild.

Then looking at Faustus, he exclaimed:

"Mighty pupil of a mightier man, if thy spirit and thy heart could entirely catch his greatness, thou wouldst still be merely reflecting the rays of his glory. But seat thyself, and let me take thy shadow."

Faustus, more and more enraged to see how infinitely the monk rated him below the Devil, now burst forth:

"Shadows! yes, indeed, shadows only hast thou seen. How darest thou thus judge and measure the human race? Hast thou seen men? Where, and how? Thou hast merely seen their shadows, which thou adornest with the tinsel of thy crazed imagination, and givest them out as the true forms. Tell me what kind of human beings thou hast seen. Were they not sectaries, fanatics, visionaries, the very offscourings of human nature? Were they not vain devotees, young wives who have cold husbands, and widows who have sleepless nights? Were they not authors eager to have every mark and pimple on their insignificant features turned into a sign and prognostication of genius? Were they not grandees, whose brilliant stations rendered their physiognomies imposing to thine eye? Thou seest that I know thy customers, and have read thy book."

Devil. Bravo, Faustus! Let me now put in a word, and tell his reverence a few mortifying truths. Brother monk, thou hast formed in thy solitary cell a phantom of perfection, and wouldst

N

fain thrust that into people's heads, which, when there, poisons the brain, as the gangrene corrupts all the flesh around it. There were men long ago who ventured to judge of the innermost of their fellow-creatures from the outside; but there was some difference between them and thee. They had travelled over a considerable part of the earth; experience had made them gray; they had lived and conversed with men, visited all the lurking holes of vice and iniquity, roved from the palace to the cot, crept into the caves of savages, and thus knew what belonged to a well-organised man, and what he could do with his faculties. But shalt thou—swollen with prejudices, pent up in a convent like a toad in the trunk of an oak— pretend to have a clear idea of that which even they barely understood?

The monk stood between the two speakers as between two volcanoes in eruption; he crossed his hands humbly upon his breast, and cried, "Have mercy!"

The Devil continued:

"Among the many impudent follies which I

observed in thy book was an attempt to draw
the Devil's portrait.   It is now high time for him
to appear to thee, in order that thou mayst correct
the likeness.   Look at me; and for once thou shalt
be able to say thou hast seen an object in its
proper form."

The Devil then appeared to him in the most
frightful of infernal figures; but he rolled a thick
mist before the eyes of Faustus, in order that he
might not blast his sight.   The monk fell to the
earth; and the Devil, resuming all his former
comeliness, exclaimed:

"Now thou mayst paint the Devil in his proper colours, provided thou hast strength.   Thou
wouldst often be thus overcome, if thou didst in
reality see the innermost of those whom thou
makest angels."

Faustus. Persist in thy folly; communicate it
to others; and by thy extravagances render religion repulsive to reasonable people.   Thou canst
not further more efficaciously the interests of the
enemy.   Farewell!

The monk had lost his senses through terror;

but he still continued writing notwithstanding his madness; and his readers never once perceived his derangement, so much did his new books resemble his old ones.

Faustus was delighted with this adventure; but becoming weary of the town, he quitted it the next morning with the Devil, and took the road to France.

CHAPTER IV.

WHEN Faustus and the Devil entered upon the
fertile soil of France, it was groaning beneath the
oppression of that cruel and cowardly tyrant
Louis the Eleventh, who was the first that ever
styled himself "the most Christian king." The
Devil had determined not to give Faustus the
slightest information beforehand concerning this
prince. He had resolved to drive him to despair,
and then overwhelm him with the most frightful
blow a mortal can receive who has rebelliously
transgressed the bounds which a powerful hand
has drawn around him.

The Devil had learnt from one of his spies that
the most Christian king was meditating a masterpiece of state policy; or, in other words, was on
the point of getting rid of his brother, the Duke
de Berry, in order that a province which had been

granted to him might revert to the crown. The
malicious fiend resolved to make Faustus a spec-
tator of this horrid scene. They rode through a
wood of oaks contiguous to a castle, and saw
among the trees a Benedictine monk, who seemed
to be telling his rosary. The Devil rejoiced
inwardly at this sight; for he read upon the
countenance of the monk that he was imploring
the Mother of God to assist him in the great
enterprise which his abbot had intrusted him
with, and likewise to save him from all danger.
This monk was Faber Vesois, confessor of the
king's brother. The Devil did not disturb him in
his pious meditations, but went on to the castle
with Faustus. They were received with all the
respect generally shown to persons of distinction
who come to visit a prince. The duke passed his
days here in the company of his beloved Monserau, thinking of no harm, and expecting no
misfortune. His agreeable manners soon gained
him the good-will of Faustus, who was delighted
to see a scion of royalty think and act like a man;
for he had been accustomed to see among the

German princes nothing but pride, coldness, and
that foolish ceremony which is only intended to
make visitors appear contemptible in their own
eyes. Some days were very pleasantly spent in
hunting and other amusements, and the prince
gained more and more upon the heart of Faustus.
The only thing that displeased him in the prince
was the weakness he displayed in regard to his
confessor, the Benedictine. He loaded him with
so much tenderness, and submitted with so much
complaisance to his will, and the monk always
looked so studiously devout, that Faustus could
not conceive how a man so frank himself could
prize such a hypocrite. The Devil, however, soon
let him into the secret by informing him of the
duke's connexion with Monserau. His love for
this fair lady was equalled by his fear of hell;
and, Madame de Monserau having a husband still
living, he was not altogether easy in respect to
his amours with her. As he neither wished to
renounce her nor expose himself to eternal punishment, he greedily caught at the baits which the
monks hang out in order to make themselves

masters of the minds of men; and when the dread
of hell tormented him too much, he allayed his
fears by receiving absolution for his sins; while
he thought it impossible for him to be too grate-
ful to a man who encouraged him to enjoy the
present, and tranquillised him in respect to the
future. "Thou seest, O Faustus," said the Devil,
"what men have made of religion. Its abuse has
often been associated with crimes and horrors, but
is nevertheless used by the wicked to cajole and
appease their rebellious consciences."

The conduct of the prince in this respect did
him little honour in the opinion of Faustus, who
had long ago parted with his own conscience, and
this last remark of the Devil's operated strongly
upon his mind; however, he permitted things to
go on in their own way, and chiefly thought of
passing his time pleasantly.

They were one evening at table in excellent
humour; the Devil was diverting the company
with his pleasant stories, and Faustus was employed in saying soft things to a pretty French
widow, who listened to him very complaisantly;

when all of a sudden, Death, in his most frightful shape, came to disturb the festival. The Benedictine caused a basket of extraordinarily large peaches, which he had just received as a present, to be brought in at dessert; and, selecting one of the finest, he offered it to the prince with a smiling and benignant air. The prince divided it with his beloved, and both ate of the peach without the slightest suspicion. They then rose from table; the monk gave his benediction to all, and hurried away. The Devil was about to commence a new story, when Madame de Monserau uttered a loud shriek. Her lovely features were distorted, her lips became blue, and the paleness of death covered her countenance. The prince rushed to her assistance; but the terrible poison began likewise to operate upon him; he fell at her feet, and cried, "Listen, O Heaven: my brother, my cruel brother, has assassinated me by the hand of that monster. He who caused his father to die of hunger in order to avoid being poisoned, has now bribed the minister of religion to poison me."

Faustus ran out of the room to seize the confessor, but he had fled; a troop of horse were waiting for him in the forest, and accompanied him in his flight. Faustus returned; but Death had seized his victims, and they had ceased to struggle with him. Faustus and the fiend instantly quitted the place.

Devil. Well, Faustus, what think you of the deed committed by the Benedictine in the name of the most Christian king?

Faustus. I am almost inclined to believe that our bodies are animated by fiendish spirits, and that we are only their instruments.

Devil. What a debasing employment for an immortal spirit to have to animate such an ill-contrived machine! Although I am a haughty demon, yet, believe me, I would rather animate a swine that wallows in the mire than one of ye, who roll in all manner of vice, and yet have the confidence to call yourselves images of the Most High.

Faustus was silent; for the adventures he was every day compelled to witness forced him, against his inclination, to believe in the moral worthlessness of man. They travelled forward, and found every where hideous monuments of the cruelty of Louis the Eleventh. Faustus frequently made use of the Devil's gold and treasure to stop the bleeding wounds which the hand of the tyrant had inflicted.

At length they arrived at Paris. Upon entering the city they found every thing in commotion. The people were rushing in crowds down one particular street; they followed the populace, and arrived in front of a scaffold covered with black cloth, and which communicated, by means of a door, with an adjoining building. Faustus asked what was the cause of all this; and he was told "that the rich Duke of Nemours was just going to be executed." "And for what?" "The king has commanded it: there is a report, indeed, that he had hostile designs against the royal house, and that he intended to murder the dauphin; but as he has only been tried in his dungeon by judges named by the king, we know nothing for certain."

"Say, rather," exclaimed another of the bystanders, "that it is his property which costs him

his life; for our sovereign, in order to make us a
great and celebrated nation, cuts off the heads of
all our wealthy men, and would serve us in the
same manner if we were to find fault with his
proceedings."

The Devil left the horses at the nearest inn,
and then led Faustus through the crowd. They
saw the duke, accompanied by his children, enter
a chamber hung round with black, where a monk
waited to receive his last confession. The father
had his eyes fixed upon his sons, and could not
look to heaven. After he had confessed himself,
he laid his trembling hands upon the heads of the
children, who were sobbing, and said, "May the
blessing of an unhappy father, who falls a victim
to tyranny and avarice, be your safeguard through
life; but, alas, ye are the heirs of misfortune.
Your rights and pretensions will infallibly doom
you to long sufferings; ye are born for misery,
and I shall die in this conviction." He wished to
say something more; but the guards silenced him,
and hurried him out upon the scaffold.

The tyrannical king had given orders that the

duke's children should be placed under the scaffold, so that the blood of their father might drop
through the boards upon their white robes. The
cries which the wretched parent uttered at the
moment his darlings were torn from him struck
terror to the hearts of all around. Tristan alone,
who was the executioner, and the king's most
intimate friend, looked on with perfect coolness,
and felt the sharpness of the axe. Faustus imagined that the groans of the unhappy parent
would excite Heaven to avenge outraged humanity. He lifted his tearful eyes towards the
bright blue sky, which seemed to smile upon the
horrid scene. For a moment he felt himself
strongly tempted to command the Devil to rescue
the duke from the hands of the executioner; but
his troubled and agitated mind was incapable of
coming to any resolution. The duke fell upon
his knees; he heard the shrieks and lamentations
of his children who were beneath the scaffold; his
own infamous death no longer occupied his mind;
he felt for the last time, and felt only for these
unfortunates; big tears hung in his eyes, his lips

trembled; the executioner gave the fatal blow, and the boiling blood of the father trickled down upon the trembling children. Bathed with paternal gore, they were then led upon the scaffold. They were shown the livid headless trunk, were made to kiss it, and then re-conducted to their prison, where they were chained up against the damp wall, so that whenever they took repose the whole weight of their bodies rested on the galling fetters. To increase their misery, their teeth were torn out from time to time.

Faustus, overwhelmed by the frightful scene he had witnessed, returned shuddering to the inn, and commanded the Devil to annihilate the tyrant who thus made a sport of human suffering.

Devil. I will not annihilate him, for that would be against the interest of hell; and why should the Devil put a stop to his cruelties when by some they are viewed with patience? If I were to further the projects of thy blind rage, who would escape thy vengeance?

Faustus. Should I not be performing a noble part, if, like unto another Hercules, I were to roam the world, and purge its thrones of such monsters?

Devil. Short-sighted man, does not your own corrupt nature prove that you must have these kings? And would not new monsters arise out of their ashes? There would then be no end of murder; the people would be divided, and thousands would fall the victims of civil war. You see here millions of bipeds like yourself, who suffer a man like themselves to despoil them of their property, to flay them alive, and to murder them at his pleasure. Did not they witness the execution of this duke, who died innocent as any lamb? Did they not gaze with pleasure, mingled with agony and grief, upon the tragic spectacle? Does not that prove they deserve their lot, and are unworthy of a better? Could they not crush the tyrant at a blow? If they have the power of relieving themselves in their own hands, wherefore should we pity their sufferings?

Here the disputation ceased.

Faustus shortly afterwards became acquainted with a gentleman of sense and education, who had

an excellent character for probity. Faustus and
the Devil pleased him so much, that he invited
them to come and pass some days with him on his
estate at a short distance from Paris, where he
lived with his family, which consisted of his wife
and his daughter, who was about sixteen years
old, and lovely as an angel. At the sight of this
divine object Faustus was like one enchanted, and
felt, for the first time, the sweet torments of delicate love. He confided his sufferings to the Devil,
who instantly offered to assist him, and laughed at
the pretended delicacy of his sentiments. Faustus
owned that it was repugnant to his feelings to
violate the laws of hospitality. The Devil replied:
"Well, Faustus, if you wish to have the gentleman's consent, I will engage to procure it. For
what do you take him?"

Faustus. For an honest man.

Devil. It is a great pity, O Faustus, that you
are so liable to deception. And so you really believe him to be an honest man! I admit that all
Paris is of the same opinion. What do you think
he loves best in the world?

Faustus. His daughter.

Devil. I know something which he loves more.

Faustus. And what is that?

Devil. Gold; and you ought to have seen that long ago. But since I have been obliged to open to thee the treasures of the earth, and thou hast had them at thy disposal, thou hast resembled the torrent which inundates the fields, caring very little where its waters flow, or where they are received. How much hast thou lost at play with this gentleman?

Faustus. Let them reckon who care more for the dross than I.

Devil. He who tricked you can tell to a ducat.

Faustus. Tricked!

Devil. Yes, tricked you. He saw how little you cared for money, and has made a noble harvest out of you. Think not that the table of this miser would be so well provided, and that he would be so prodigal of the richest wines, and that thou wouldst see so many guests around him, provided thy gold did not work these miracles. At every moment he trembles lest we should leave

o

his house. I see by thy astonishment that thou hast been a spendthrift all thy life, and that thou hast never felt this thirst for gold, which can extinguish all the desires of the heart, and even the most pressing wants of nature. Follow me, but tread softly.

They descended a staircase, went through several subterranean passages, and came at last to an iron door. The Devil then said to Faustus: "Look through the key-hole." Faustus perceived in a vault, illumined by the feeble light of a lamp, the gentleman seated by the side of a strong-box, in which were many sacks of money, which he was looking at with tenderness. He then flung the money he had won from Faustus into another box, and wept because he saw there was not sufficient to fill it. The Devil said softly to Faustus: "For the sum which is wanting to fill that box, he will sell thee his daughter."

Faustus was incredulous. The Devil waxed wroth, and said impatiently:

"I will show thee that gold has such irresistible power over the minds of men, that even

at this moment some fathers and mothers belonging to the village are in the neighbouring
wood selling for money their babes and sucklings to the emissaries of the king, although
they are well aware that the poor little things
are destined to be slaughtered, in order that the
king may drink their blood, with the foolish hope
of renovating and refreshing the corrupt tide
which flows in his own veins.

Faustus (*with a shudder*). Then the world
is worse than hell, and I shall quit it without
regret. But I will be convinced with my own
eyes before I credit any thing so horrible.

They now went into the wood, and concealed
themselves among the bushes, where they perceived the emissaries of the king in conference
with some men and women, and the priest of the
parish. Four little children were stretched upon
the grass, one of them crying pitiably. The
mother lifted it up and gave it pap, in order to
quiet it; whilst the others crept upon the ground,
and played with the flowers. The emissaries
counted money into the hands of the husbands;

the priest had his share, and the children were
delivered up. The echoes of the wood repeated
for a long time the cries of the little wretches as
they were carried away. The mothers groaned;
but the men said to them, " Here is gold; let us
go to the public-house and buy wine, and drink
to a fresh offspring. It is better that the king
should eat the brats now they are young than
flay them when they are old, or tie them up in a
sack and fling them into the Seine. It would
have been much better for us if we had been devoured as soon as we were born."

The priest comforted them, and said :

" They had done a meritorious act, and one
which was pleasing to the Mother of God, to
whom the king was entirely devoted." He added,
" that subjects were born for the king; and that,
as he reigned upon earth as Heaven's vicege-
rent, he had a right to dispose of them according to his pleasure. and that they were bound
to revere the slightest of his fancies as a sacred
law."

The peasants then went to the public-house,

where they spent half the blood-money in drink,
and kept the rest to pay the king's taxes.

The Devil now looked at Faustus with an air
of mockery, and said, "Hast thou still doubts
whether the gentleman will sell thee his daughter? Thou at least wilt not eat her."

Faustus. I swear by the black hell which at
this moment appears to me a paradise when compared with the earth, that I will henceforward give
boundless scope to all my passions, and, by ra-
vaging and destroying, believe that I am acting
consistently to such a monster as man. Fly, and
purchase me his daughter: she is doomed to destruction, as is every thing that breathes.

This was exactly the disposition in which the
Devil had long been desirous to see Faustus,
in order that he might precipitate him to the
end of his career, and thereby ease himself of a
grievous burden, and cease to be the slave of a
thing so contemptible as man was in his eyes.
That very evening he began to sound the father;
and the next morning, whilst they walked together, he made proposals to him, and showed

him gold and jewels, which the miser gazed at with rapture; but which, however, he would not take until he had made a parade of his virtue. At every objection the old hypocrite started, the Devil augmented the sum; and at last he bade so high that the miser accepted it, after much ceremony, laughing secretly at the madman who flung away his gold so foolishly. The contract was made, and the father led Faustus to his daughter; and as he could prove that her parent was a consenting party, she fell a willing victim.

The father in the mean time went with his gold and a lamp to the vault where he kept his treasure, and which was known to none of his family. He was overjoyed in having obtained sufficient to fill his second strong-box. From fear of being followed, he closed the door hastily behind him, forgetting that it went with a spring-lock, and that he had left the key on the outside. The lamp was extinguished by the wind of the door, and he found himself suddenly involved in profound darkness. The air of the vault was

thick and damp, and he soon felt a difficulty in
his respiration. He now first perceived that he
had not the key with him, and death-like anguish
shot coldly through his heart. He had still
strength and instinct sufficient to find his box;
he laid the gold in it, and staggered back to the
door, where he considered whether he should cry
out or not. He was cruelly agitated by the al-
ternative of discovering his secret, or of making
this vault his tomb. But his cries would have
been to no purpose; for the cavern had no connexion with the inhabited part of the house, and
he had always so well chosen his time, that no
one had ever yet seen him when he crept to the
worship of his idol. After having for a long
time struggled with himself, without coming to
any resolution, the terrible images which assailed
his imagination, joined to the thickness of the
air, totally disordered his brain. He sunk to
the earth, and rolling himself to the spot where
his box stood, he hugged it in his arms, and
became raving mad. He struggled with despair
and death at the moment of the ruin of his

daughter, whose innocence he had bartered for
gold. Some days after, when all the corners of
the house had been closely searched, chance led
a servant to the cavern; it was opened, and the
unfortunate wretch was found lying, a blue and
ghastly corpse, upon his dear-bought treasure.
The Devil informed Faustus upon their return
to Paris of the issue of this affair, and Faustus
believed that, on this occasion, Providence had
justified itself.

The fiend having learnt that the Parliament
were about to decide upon a case unexampled
and disgraceful to humanity, he thought it ad-
visable that Faustus should hear it. The fact
was this: a surgeon, returning late one night to
Paris with his faithful servant, heard, not far
from the highway, the groans and lamentations
of a man. His heart led him to the spot, where
he found a murderer broken alive upon the wheel,
who conjured him, in the name of God, to put an
end to his existence. The surgeon shuddered
with horror and fright; but recovering himself,
he thought whether it would not be possible for

him to reset the bones of this wretch, and preserve his life. He spoke a few words to his servant, took the murderer from the wheel, and laid him gently in the chaise. He then carried him to his house, where he undertook his cure, which he at last accomplished. He had been informed that the Parliament had offered a reward of one hundred louis-d'ors to any one who would discover the person who had taken the assassin from the wheel. He told the murderer of this when he sent him away, and, giving him money, he advised him not to stay in Paris. The very first thing which this monster did was to go to the Parliament and betray his benefactor, for the sake of the hundred louis-d'ors. The cheeks of the judges, which so seldom change colour, became pallid at this denunciation; for he informed them with the greatest effrontery that he was the very assassin, who, having been broken alive upon the place where he had committed the murder, had been saved by the compassion of the surgeon. The latter was sent for; and the Devil conducted Faustus into the hall of judgment exactly at the

moment he appeared. The attorney-general informed the surgeon of what he was accused; but
the surgeon, being certain of his servant's fidelity,
stoutly denied the charge. He was advised to
confess, because a most convincing witness could
be brought against him. He bade them produce
him. A side-door opened, and the murderer
stepped coolly into the court, and, looking the
surgeon full in the face, undauntedly repeated his
accusation, without forgetting a single circumstance. The surgeon shrieked, "O monster! what
can have urged thee to this horrible ingratitude?"

Murderer. The hundred louis-d'ors, which you
told me of when you sent me away. Did you
think that I was satisfied with merely recovering
the use of my limbs? I was broken alive on the
wheel for a murder which I committed for ten
crowns, and I was not fool enough to lose gain-
ing a hundred louis without running any risk.

Surgeon. Thou wretch! thy cries and groans
touched my heart. I took thee down from the
wheel, comforted thee, and bound up thy wounds.
I fed thee with mine own hand, till thou couldst

use thy shattered joints. I gave thee money, which thou canst not yet have spent. I discovered to thee, from regard to thy own safety, the reward which had been offered by the Parliament; and I swear to thee, by Heaven above, that if thou hadst told me of thy devilish intention, I would have sold my last rag, and have furnished thee with the sum, in order that so horrible a piece of ingratitude might remain for ever unknown to the world. Gentlemen, judge between me and him; I confess myself guilty.

President. You have greviously offended justice by endeavouring to preserve the life of him whom the law, for the common safety, had condemned to die; but for this once strict justice shall be silent, and humanity only shall sit in judgment. The hundred louis-d'ors shall be yours, and the murderer shall be again broken upon the wheel.

Faustus, who during the whole of this strange trial had been snorting like a madman, gave now such a thundering huzza, that the whole gallery echoed. The Devil, who observed that the last

impression was about to destroy the first, soon
led him to another scene.

Some surgeons, doctors of medicine, and natu-
ralists had formed a secret society, for the purpose
of inquiring into the mechanism of the human
body, and the effect of the soul upon matter.   In
order to satisfy their curiosity, they inveigled,
under all sorts of pretences, poor men and women
into a house at some distance from the city, the
upper part of which was constructed in such a
manner that it was impossible to discover from
without what was going forward within.   Having
tied their victims with strong cords down upon
a long table, and having placed a gag in their
mouths, they then removed their skin and their
flesh, and laid bare their muscles, their nerves,
their hearts, and their brains.   In order to come·
at what they sought, they fed the wretches with
strengthening broths, and caused them to die
slowly under the slashing of their knives and
lancets.   The Devil knew that they intended this
night to assemble, and said to Faustus, "Thou
hast seen a surgeon, who, for the sake of humanity,

or for love of his art, cured an assassin whom justice had broken on the wheel; I will now show thee physicians, who, in pursuit of secrets which they will not discover, skin their fellow-creatures alive. Thou appearest incredulous! Follow me, and I will convince thee. We will represent two doctors."

He led him to a solitary house. They entered the laboratory, which the rays of the sun never penetrated. Here they saw the surgeons dissecting a miserable being, whose flesh quivered beneath their fratricidal hands, and whose bosom heaved with the most painful agony. They were so engaged with their object, that they never once perceived the Devil and Faustus. The latter, feeling his nerves thrill with horror, rushed out, struck his forehead with his hand, and commanded the fiend to tear down the house upon their heads, and bury them and their deed beneath its ruins.

Devil. Why this rage, O Faustus? Dost thou not perceive that thou art acting, in respect to the moral world, in the same manner as they act in regard to the physical world? They mangle the flesh of the living; and thou, by my destructive hand, exercisest thy fury upon the whole creation.

Faustus. Outcast fiend! dost thou think my heart is made of stone? Dost thou think that I can see unmoved the torments of yon poor flayed and butchered wretch? But if I can neither dry his tears nor cure his wounds, I can avenge him, and put him out of pain. Away! away! do as I have bid thee, or dread my wrath!

The Devil obeyed with pleasure. He shook the house to its foundation, and down it toppled with a hideous noise, and overwhelmed the wicked doctors. Faustus hurried to Paris, without attending to the look of wild exultation which the Devil cast upon him.

Faustus, having heard much talk of the prisons which the most Christian king had caused to be built for the purpose of receiving those whom he dreaded, had a strong desire to see the interior of them. The Devil willingly undertook to satisfy his curiosity; and although the guards were forbidden, under pain of death, to permit any strangers to enter these habitations of horror, yet

the golden arguments which the Devil used procured him and his companion a ready admittance.
They saw there cages of iron, in which it was impossible for a man to stand upright, or sit down,
or place himself in any easy posture. The wretches
who were compelled to tenant these iron dwell-
ings had their limbs galled by heavy chains. The
keeper said, confidentially, that when the king
was in good health, he frequently walked in the
gallery, in order to enjoy the song of his nightin-
gales; for thus did he call these wretched victims.
Faustus asked some of the unfortunates the cause
of their captivity; and he heard stories which
pierced him to the heart. At last, coming to a
cage wherein was a venerable-looking old man,
he put the same question to him, and the prisoner
answered, in a plaintive tone:

"Whoever you are, let my sad story serve
you as a warning never to assist a tyrant in his
cruelties. You behold in me the Bishop of Verdun, who first gave to the king the idea of these
horrible cages, and was the very first to be shut
up in one of them after they were completed.

Here have I, for fourteen years, done penance for my sins, praying daily to God to end my torments by death."

Faustus. Ha, ha ! Your excellence, then, like another Perillus, has found a Phalaris. Do you know that story ? You shake your head. Well, I will tell it you.

" This Perillus, who was neither a bishop nor a Christian, constructed a brazen bull, which he showed to the tyrant Phalaris as a masterpiece of invention, and assured him that it was constructed in such a manner, that, if his majesty would shut up a man in it, and then heat it red-hot by a fire laid beneath it, the shrieks of the tormented man would exactly resemble the bellowings of a bull, which would doubtless afford his majesty great pleasure. 'My dear Perillus,' said the tyrant, 'I am much indebted to you ; but it is right that the artist should prove his own work.' He then made Perillus creep into the beast's belly ; and when the fire was laid beneath it, he did in reality bellow like a bull. Thus did Phalaris, a thousand years ago, play very much the same part with

Perillus which the most Christian king has been playing with you, most reverend Bishop of Verdun."

Bishop. I wish I had heard this story twenty years ago; I should then have taken warning from it.

Faustus. You see that history may sometimes be useful, even to a bishop. I weep for the fate of your companions in misery; but I laugh at yours.

Faustus wished now to see this king, whose horrible deeds had so heated his imagination, that he could hardly represent him to himself under a human figure. The Devil told him that it would be impossible for them in their present forms to enter the Castle of Plessis du Parc, where cowardice and fear kept the tyrant a prisoner. He added, that no one, with the exception of some necessary domestics, the physician, the confessor, and one or two astrologers, could enter without a particular order.

Faustus. Then let us assume other figures and dresses.

P

Devil. Good; I will instantly remove two of his guards, and we will do their duty. This is an excellent time to see the tyrant. The fear of death is already avenging upon his cowardly spirit the thousands whom he has slaughtered. Day and night he only thinks of putting off the moment which is to terminate his existence, and death seems to him more hideous every second. . I will make you a witness of his torments.

The Devil instantly put his project into execution, and they found themselves standing sentinels in the interior of the castle, where reigned the mournful silence of the tomb. Thither had he, before whom millions trembled, banished himself, in order to escape from the vengeance of the relations of the murdered. Although he could thus fly from the sight of his subjects, he could not escape the cutting remorse of his own heart, nor the pains of his emaciated body. In vain did he implore Heaven to grant him health and repose ; in vain did he attempt to bribe it by presents to saints, to priests, and to churches ; in vain did he cover himself with

relics from all parts of the world : that frightful
sentence, *thou shalt die*, seemed always ringing
in his ears. He scarcely ventured to move out
of his chamber, lest he should find an assassin
in one of those whom he might meet. If anguish drove him into the free air, he went armed
with lance and dagger, just as if he had strength
to use either. Four hundred guards watched
day and night around the stronghold of the half-
dead monster; three times every hour did their
hoarse calls, echoing from post to post, break
the solemn stillness, and remind the tyrant of
the flight of time. All around his castle gibbets
were erected ; and the hangman, Tristan, his
only true friend, went about the country every
day, and returned at night with fresh victims,
in order, by their execution, to diminish the
fears of the tyrant, who from time to time
would walk in an apartment which was only
separated from the torture-room by a thin par-
tition. There he listened to the groans and
shrieks of the wretches on the rack, and found
in the sufferings of others a slight alleviation

of his own. Wearing on his hat a leaden image
of the Virgin,—his pretended protectress,—he
drank the blood of murdered sucklings, and allowed himself to be tormented by his physician,
whom he requited with ten thousand crowns a
month.

This was the wretch whom Faustus saw ; and
his heart rejoiced when he contemplated the
paleness of his cheeks, and the furrows which
anguish and despair had made in his brow.
He was on the point of leaving this abode of
monotonous horror, when the Devil whispered
him to remain until the next day, and he would
see a singular spectacle. The king had heard
that a hermit lived in Calabria, who was honoured as a saint through all Sicily. This fool
had, from his fourteenth to his fortieth year,
dwelt upon a naked rock, where, exposed to the
rains and tempests of heaven, he martyred his
body by stripes and fasting, and refused his mind
all cultivation. But, the rays of sanctity concealing his stupidity, he soon saw the prince and
the peasant at his feet. Louis had requested the

King of Sicily to send him this creature, because
he hoped to be cured by him. The hermit was
now on the road; and as he brought with him
the holy oil of Rheims, to anoint the tyrant's
body, the latter imagined that all his disorders
would soon vanish, and he should become young
again. The happy day arrived: the Calabrian
boor approached the castle; the king received him
at the gate, fell at his feet, and asked him for
life and health. The Calabrian played his part
in so ridiculous a manner, that Faustus could
not avoid laughing aloud at the farce. Tristan
and his myrmidons were advancing to seize
him, and he would doubtlessly have paid for
laughing with his life, had not the Devil rescued him from their claws, and flown away
with him. When they arrived at Paris, Faustus
said:

"Is it by this contemptible, superstitious,
tottering object, that the bold sons of France
allow themselves to be enslaved? He is a mere
skeleton in purple, who can scarcely cough out
of his asthmatic throat the desire to live; yet

they tremble before him, as if he were a giant,
whose terrible arms could encircle the whole
earth. When the lion, enfeebled by age, lies
languishing in his den, the most insignificant
beasts of the forests are not afraid of him, but
approach and mock the fallen tyrant."

Devil. It is this which chiefly distinguishes
the king of men from the king of beasts. The
latter is only formidable as long as he can use
his own strength; but the former, who binds the
strength of his slaves to his will, is as powerful
when lying on the bed of sickness, as when, in
the vigour of health, he is at the head of his
armies. Are you not now convinced that men
are only guided by folly, which dooms them to
be slaves? Break their chains to-day, and they
would forge themselves others to-morrow. Do
what you can, they will always go on in the same
eternal circle, and are condemned for ever to seize
the shadow for the reality.

The Devil, having shown Faustus all that was
remarkable in and about the capital of France,
took him to Calais; and, crossing the Channel,

they arrived in London at the very moment
that hideous abortion, the Duke of Gloucester,
made himself Protector of the kingdom, and
was endeavouring to take away the crown from
the children of his brother, the late king. He
had removed the father by means of poison, and
had already persuaded the queen (who, upon the
first discovery of his projects, had fled for refuge,
with her children, to Westminster Sanctuary) to
deliver up to him the youthful heir of the throne,
together with his brother York. Faustus was
present when Doctor Shaw, by the command of
the Protector, informed the astonished people
from the pulpit, that the yet living mother of
the duke and the deceased king had admitted
various lovers ; that the late king was the
offspring of such adultery ; and that no one of
the royal line, except the Protector, could boast
of a legitimate birth. He saw those noblemen
executed who would not accede to the execrable
plot ; and the Devil conducted him into the
Tower at the very moment when Tyrrell and his
assistant murdered the lawful king and his bro-

ther, and buried them beneath the threshold of
the dungeon. He was a witness of the base
submission of the Parliament, and of the coronation of the frightful tyrant. He witnessed the
negotiation of the queen to support the murderer
of her sons in his usurped throne, by giving him
the hand of her eldest daughter, in order that
she herself might still retain a shadow of so-
vereignty; although at the same time she had
entered into a secret alliance with the Earl of
Richmond, who was destined to be her avenger.
Faustus felt himself so enraged, that not all the
charms of the blooming Englishwomen could
keep him any longer in this cursed isle, which
he quitted with hatred and disgust; for neither
in Germany nor in France had he seen crimes
committed with so much coolness and impunity.
When they were on the point of embarking, the
Devil said to him :

"These people will groan for a time beneath
the yoke of despotism; they will then sacrifice
one of their kings upon the scaffold of freedom, in
order that they may sell themselves to his suc-

cessors for gold and titles. In hell there is very little respect paid to these gloomy islanders, who would suck the marrow from all the carcasses in the universe, if they thought to find gold in the bones. They boast of their morality, and despise all other nations; yet if you were to place what you call virtue in one scale, and vice, with twopence, in the other, they would forget their morality, and pocket the money. They talk of their honour and integrity, but never enter into a treaty but with a firm resolution of breaking it as soon as a farthing is to be gained by so doing. After death, they inhabit the most pestilential marsh of the kingdom of darkness, and their souls are scourged without mercy. None of the other damned will have any communication with them. If the inhabitants of the Continent could do without sugar and coffee, the sons of proud England would soon return to the state in which they were when Julius Cæsar, Canute of Denmark, or William the Conqueror, did them the honour to invade their island."

Faustus. For a devil, thou knowest history passably well.

Hereupon he led him to Milan, where they saw the Duke Galeas Sforza murdered on St. Stephen's day in the cathedral; Faustus having previously heard the assassins loudly beseeching St. Stephen and St. Ambrose to inspire them with the courage necessary for so noble a deed.

In Florence, the seat of the Muses, they saw the nephew of the great Cosmo, the father of his country, murdered in the church of Santa Reparata, at the altar, just at the moment when the priest raised the host in his hands; for the Archbishop of Florence, Salviati, had informed the murderers that this was to be the signal. He had been bribed to assist in this enterprise by the Pope, who was determined to annihilate the Medicis, in order to rule sole sovereign in Italy.

In the north of Europe they saw wild barbarians and drunken ruffians murdering and pillaging like the more civilised Europeans. In Spain they found upon the throne deceit and hypocrisy wearing the mask of religion. They

saw, at an *auto-da-fè*, men and women immolated
in the flames to the mild Deity of the Christians;
and they heard the grand inquisitor, Torquemada,
boast to Ferdinand and Isabella that, since the
establishment of the holy tribunal, it had tried
eighty thousand suspected persons, and had burnt
six thousand convicted heretics. When Faustus
first saw the ladies and cavaliers assembled in the
grand square, dressed in their richest habits, he
imagined that he had come just in time for some
joyous festival; but when he heard the condemned
wretches howling and lamenting in the midst of
a mob of monks who were at their devotions, he
was convinced that religion, when misused, makes
man the most execrable monster on the earth.
He, however, began to imagine that all these
horrors were the necessary consequences of man's
nature, who is an animal that must either tear
his fellow-creatures to pieces, or be torn to pieces
by them.

The Devil, perceiving that Faustus was amazed
and confounded by these scenes, said to him:

" Thou seest how the courts of Europe resemble each other in wickedness and crime. Let us now go to Rome, and see whether the ecclesiastical government goes on better."

The malicious Leviathan flattered himself that Alexander the Sixth, who wore at that time the triple crown, and held in his hands the keys of heaven and of hell, would give the finishing blow to the harassed spirit of Faustus, and would enable him to return below with his victim. For a long time he had been weary of staying on the earth; for although he had in the course of many thousand years so often traversed it, he still saw merely the same beings and the same actions. From this we may learn that there is something so annoying in uniformity, that even the wild horrors of Satan's hall are to be preferred to it.

On the way to Rome they passed by two hostile armies encamped face to face. The one was commanded by Malatesta of Rimini, the other by a papal general. The crafty Alexander was now endeavouring, either by poisoning, secret assassination, or open war, to deprive all the

Italian noblemen of their property, in order that
he might convert their castles and domains into
principalities for his illegitimates. He began with
the weakest, and had despatched this little army
to eject Malatesta from his fief of Rimini. Faustus and the Devil, riding along the road, perceived upon an eminence contiguous to the papal
camp two men, magnificently dressed, engaged in
a furious combat. Moved by curiosity, Faustus
advanced to the spot; the fiend followed him; and
they perceived, by the rage of the antagonists,
that nothing less than the death of one of them
would end the struggle. But what appeared to
Faustus most extraordinary was a milk-white
goat, adorned with ribbons of various colours,
which a page seemed to hold as the prize of victory, as he stood, with the utmost coolness, near
the two raging warriors. Many cavaliers had assembled upon the height, and awaited the issue of
the affair. Faustus approached one of them, and
asked, with his German simplicity, whether the
gentlemen were fighting for that handsome goat.
He had observed that the two champions, when-

ever they paused to take breath, looked at the goat with much tenderness, and each seemed, according to knightly custom, to entreat it to assist him in his danger. The Italian, turning to Faustus, coolly answered, " Yes, certainly; and I hope our general will punish with death the audacious knight who dared to remove from his tent the handsomest goat in the world, at the time he was gone to reconnoitre the enemy's camp." Faustus stepped back, shook his head, and scarcely knew whether he was dreaming or awake. The Devil let him remain for some time in this perplexity; he then took him aside, and whispered certain things in his ear, which made Faustus blush, and which will not bear repetition. The duel in the mean time went on as hotly as ever, until the sword of the papal general found an opening in the knight's mail, and laid him wallowing in blood upon the ground. He yielded up his soul amidst curses and imprecations, and took, with his last look, a tender farewell of the pretty animal. The general was congratulated by the surrounders, and the page delivered him the goat. He called it "his dearest, his best-beloved," and loaded it with the most tender caresses.

Faustus departed from the place of combat, and was hesitating between a desire to laugh and a feeling of disgust, when the Devil said to him:

"This duel has made thee acquainted with the papal general; but he who commands the hostile army does not deserve thy attention less. The one has risked his life for love of a white goat; and the other has already poisoned and strangled with his own hand, in order that he might get possession of their property, two of his wives, sprung from the best families in Italy. He is now on the point of marrying a third; and she will, in all probability, experience the same fate. Both of these personages are otherwise very religious men,—attend processions, make vows to Heaven, and implore it for assistance. For which side do you think it will now declare?"

Faustus gave the Devil a wild look, and left the malicious question unanswered; but the Devil, who wished to punish him for having formerly boasted of the moral worth of man, failed

not to make some bitter jokes upon the amours
of the papal general and the conjugal tenderness
of Malatesta of Rimini.

The sight of Rome and its majestic ruins,
over which the mighty spirit of the old Romans
seemed yet to hover, filled Faustus with wonder;
and, as he was well acquainted with the history
of those lords of the ancient world, the remembrance of their heroic actions elevated his soul
to a pitch of enthusiasm. But the modern inhabitants of this celebrated city soon inspired him
with very different sentiments. By the Devil's
advice, they announced themselves as German
noblemen, whom curiosity to see the magnificence
of Rome had brought there. But their retinue,
their pomp, and their demeanour, caused a suspicion to be entertained that they were of more
consequence than they pretended to be. Friars
and matrons, quacks and harlequins, flocked
to them, as soon as the noise of their arrival had
echoed through all the haunts of those who get
their livelihood by administering to the crimes
and the weaknesses of men. They offered them

their several female relations, and depicted their charms and various attractions with such fiery eloquence, that Faustus, besieged on every side, knew not which to prefer. As these wretches uttered religious maxims in the same breath with the most stimulant descriptions of voluptuousness, Faustus imagined himself authorised in believing that they merely made use of religion to appease the cravings of passion, revolted by their shameful deeds and wickedness.

The next day after their arrival, Faustus and the Devil were invited to dinner by the Cardinal Cæsar Borgia, one of the many illegitimates of the Pope. He received them in the most splendid manner, and promised to introduce them to his holiness. They went on horseback, attended by a retinue of servants, to the Vatican, and Faustus and the Devil kissed the toe of the Pope: the German performed this act of devotion with all the fervour of a good Christian Catholic; but the Devil muttered to himself, "If Alexander knew who I am, I should, most probably, see him at my own feet." After the usual ceremonies were over, the Pope invited them into his private apartments, where he spoke to them very freely, and made them acquainted with his other illegitimates, the famous Lucretia; Francisco Borgia, Duke of Candia, &c.

The Pope found the society of the handsome and well-made Leviathan so much to his liking, that, from the first interview, he showed him particular favour, which grew at length, as we shall see, to the closest intimacy. Faustus attached himself to Cardinal Borgia, who gave him such a glowing description of the pleasures and temptations of Rome, that he hardly knew whether he was in the Vatican or in the Temple of Venus. The Cardinal made him more nearly acquainted with his sister, who was married to Alphonso of Arragon. This siren displayed voluptuousness and sensuality in a form and face so attractive and charming, that Faustus stood before her like one enchanted.

Faustus and the Devil went one evening to the Vatican to see a play, which astonished the young German more than any thing he had yet seen at

the papal court. It was the *Mandragola* which
was represented. The noble Machiavel had composed this licentious and satirical piece, in order
to lay before the eyes of the court of Rome a
striking picture of the boundless corruption of
the clergy, and to prove that to be the sole cause·
of the dissolute lives of the laity. But he deceived himself in his honourable design : the
Mandragola was applauded, not on account of its
morality, which was not understood, but of its
licentiousness. Faustus heard the Pope and the
cardinals, the nuns and the ladies, praising certain things which, in his opinion, the most dissolute of the Roman emperors would not have
permitted upon their theatre. But real scenes yet
more abominable soon put an end to his astonishment; and he perceived that the actions of Alexander and his children infinitely surpassed all
that which the annals of the human race had
hitherto consigned to infamy and abhorrence.
Lucretia was pleased yet more by Faustus's rich
presents than his fine face and form. By this
intimate connexion with her, he discovered her

incestuous intercourse with her two brothers, the
Cardinal and Francisco; which she also extended
to the Pope her father. The only one whom
she treated ill was Alphonso, who had the honour
to be her spouse. Faustus now guessed the cause
of the implacable hatred which the Cardinal entertained against his brother Francisco: it arose
from jealousy at his sister's preferring the latter
to himself; and he often swore to take vengeance
upon his brother.

It was the custom of Faustus, after having
the whole day wallowed in the shameful pleasures of the court and city, to pester the Devil's
ears with complaints of the wickedness of men.
He was shocked at their crimes, although he
himself had neither strength nor desire to resist
any of his inclinations. He generally concluded
his sermonising by asking, "How could such a
monster ever have been elected Pope?"

The Devil, who perfectly knew how that event
had been brought about (for one of the princes
of hell had been at the election), would tell him
how "Alexander bought up the votes of the

cardinals by magnificent promises; and being called upon, after his installation, to fulfil them, he either banished or caused to be privately assassinated all those who had any claims upon him."

Faustus. I can easily conceive that the cardinals were sufficiently corrupt to make him Pope; but how the people can submit to his decrees is beyond my comprehension.

Devil. The Romans are perfectly content with him. He protects the populace, and ravages and pillages the great. Can they wish for a better Pope than one who sanctifies their crimes by his own example; and who, besides the indulgences he distributes, shows by his actions that men have no reason to be terrified at any crime?

The Pope having, at a consistorial court, elevated his eldest illegitimate, Francisco, to the dignity of General of the Papal See, the Cardinal instantly formed the Christian resolution of putting his brother out of the way, and thereby opening a more extensive field to his own ambition. Vanosa, his mother, had informed him that the Pope intended to raise a throne for Francisco upon the ruin of the Italian princes; and through him, as his eldest-born, execute all the projects which he had formed for the prosperity and aggrandisement of his family. The Cardinal, who had always certain assassins in his pay, sent for his faithful Dom Michelotto, and thus addressed him:

"Brave and honest Michelotto, five years have already passed since the accession of my father to the papal chair, and I am not yet what I might have been, had I acted with less delicacy and more prudence. He first made me an archbishop, and now I am become a cardinal; but what is that for a spirit which burns with a desire to distinguish itself, and which aspires to glory! My revenues scarcely supply me with absolute necessaries, and it is impossible for me to reward, according to the wish of my heart, those friends who have rendered me essential services. Art thou not, O Michelotto, a striking example of it thyself? Have I been able to acquit myself

towards thee in the manner which my obligations
to thee demand? But shall we always languish
in this shameful inactivity; and shall we wait till
fortune or chance do something for those who will
do nothing for themselves? Dost thou think that
the monotonous life I lead in the conclave and in
the church was intended for a spirit like mine?
Am I born for all these ridiculous and superstitious ceremonies? If nature had not by foolish
caprice brought my brother into the world before
me, would not all those situations, all those hon-
ours, by which men are alone enabled to perform
great actions, have fallen to my lot? Does my
brother know how to profit by the advantages
which the Pope and blind Fortune fling in his
way? Let me once occupy his place, and my
name shall soon resound through all Europe.
Nature stamped me for a hero, and him for a
priest; therefore I must seek to repair the negli-
gence of Fortune if I wish to fulfil my destiny.
Compare him and me, and who will say we are
sprung from the same father? But be he my
brother—and it little matters; for the man who

wishes to rise above the rest should forget tenderness and relationship—those puny bonds of nature—and should not hesitate to dip his hands in the sacrifice of any one whose existence may be an obstacle to his noble views. It is thus that all great men act; it is thus that the founder of immortal Rome acted. In order that Rome might arrive at the height of grandeur to which his genius wished to carry it, he did not hesitate to stab his brother; and, in order that Cæsar Borgia may attain immortality, his brother Francisco must bleed beneath thy knife, most courageous Michelotto. Yes; for although it would be easy for me, in the darkness of the night, to assassinate him myself and remain unsuspected, I reserve for thee this deed, in order that thou mayst have a greater right to share with me my grandeur and my future fortunes. To-morrow I shall go to Naples to assist, in quality of legate, at the coronation of the king. Vanosa, my mother, who, between you and me, is weary of seeing her enterprising Cæsar a cardinal, gives this evening a supper to myself, my brother, and a few friends.

Francisco will go late at night to an assignation
in which he and I mutually share; and I ill
know Michelotto if ever he finds his way back to
his palace. My name is Cæsar, and I will be all
or nothing."

Michelotto grasped the cardinal's hand, thanked
him for his confidence, assured him of his fidelity,
and went his way in order to get some of his
companions to assist him in the affair.

Faustus and the Devil were also invited to the
supper. Gaiety reigned among the guests. The
good-natured Francisco loaded his brother with
caresses, which, however, did not shake his resolution. When they rose from table, Cæsar took
leave of his mother, and said he must now go
to the Pope and receive his orders for Naples.
The two brothers walked with each other a little
way, followed by Faustus and the Devil. Francisco soon took leave of his brother, having first
told him where he was going. The Cardinal, with
a smiling air, wished him much pleasure: hurry-
ing to the Vatican, he finished his business there,
and then went to the rendezvous, where he found

Michelotto and his ruffians, whom he directed
how to proceed. Faustus had not the slightest
suspicion of what was going forward; but the
Devil, who knew when the horrible drama was
to conclude, transported him to the banks of the
Tiber at the very moment Michelotto and his
assistants flung into the stream the corpse of the
murdered Francisco. Faustus would have attacked
the assassins, though he was still ignorant who
their victim was; but the Devil prevented him,
and said:

"Do not approach; keep thyself quiet, and let
none of those people see thee; they swarm so at
Rome and at the Vatican, that thou wouldst not
be safe, even at my side, if they were to perceive
that thou didst observe them. The murdered
man whom they flung into the water is Francisco
Borgia, Duke of Candia; his murderer is his
brother, and what thou seest now is only the pre-.
lude to actions which will astonish hell itself and
make it tremble."

He then discovered to him the whole of the
plot, and repeated to him the Cardinal's conversa-

tion with Michelotto. Faustus replied, with more coolness than the Devil expected :

" Their deeds will not astonish me, however infamous they may be ; for what else can we expect from a family where the father lives in incest with his daughter, and the brothers with their sister ? But henceforth I will never suffer any one to boast in my presence of the moral worth of man ; for, in comparison with man, especially if he be a priest, the worst fiend is innocent as an angel. Oh, why was I not born in happy Arabia, where I might have passed my solitary existence, with a palm-tree for my shelter, and with Nature for my god !"

The body of Francisco being found in the Tiber, his assassination was soon noised about Rome and through all Italy. The Pope was so afflicted at the intelligence, that he abandoned himself to the most frightful despair, and remained three days without eating or drinking ; but he did not forget to offer immense rewards for the discovery of the murderers. His daughter, who guessed from whence the blow came, gave her mother intelligence of the severe intentions of the Pope; and Vanosa, at dead of night, went to the Vatican. The Devil, who, in quality of favourite, had remained alone with his holiness whilst his affliction was at its height, hastened away upon the appearance of Vanosa; and having found Faustus, who was consoling the lovely Lucretia, he led him to the door of the Pope's apartment, where they heard the following dialogue.

"A fratricide! a cardinal!—and thou, mother of them both, dost tell me this with as much coolness as if Cæsar had merely poisoned one of the Colonnas or Orsinis. He has, in murdering his brother, destroyed his own fame, and has undermined the foundation of that monument of grandeur which I was about to raise. But the monster shall not escape punishment; he shall feel my vengeance."

Vanosa. Rodrigo Borgia, thou hast shared the couch of my mother and myself, and wast the first that dishonoured Lucretia, my daughter and thine. Who can number all those whom thou

hast secretly poisoned and assassinated? Yet thou
art not less a pope. Rome trembles before thee,
and all Christianity adores thee. Every thing
depends upon the situation in which men are
when they commit crimes. I am the mother of
both, Rodrigo, and I knew that Cæsar would
murder Francisco.

Pope. Thou wretch!

Vanosa. Am I? If I be, I have become so in
thy school. It was right that the timorous and
gentle Francisco should give place to the fiery,
the enterprising Cæsar, in order that the glittering hopes may be fulfilled which thou didst
confide to me upon thy elevation to the papal
chair. Francisco was intended by nature to be
a monk; my Cæsar to be a conqueror—and I call
him so already in prophetic spirit. He alone has
power to annihilate the great and petty tyrants of
Italy, and to win himself a crown. Appoint him
standard-bearer to the papal see, and he will
make the Borgias kings of the Italian realms. Is
not this thy most ardent wish? All thy poisonings and murders will have been to no more pur-

pose if Cæsar remains a cardinal, than they would
have been if yon feeble driveller had lived. Only
from Cæsar can I expect protection when thou art
no more. He loves his mother; but the other
boy neglected me, and only flattered thee, from
whom he expected his greatness. Cæsar feels
that a woman like me, who could bring forth a
hero, can likewise point out to him the way to
immortal deeds. Brighten up, Rodrigo, and be
wise; for know that the hand which dispatched
thy favourite was directed by a daring spirit, who
would not hesitate to take thy own life wert thou
to remove the veil which has been flung over this
deed of necessity.

Pope. The solidity of thy arguments restores
me to myself, and thy eloquence exalts my soul,
although it makes me shudder. Francisco is
dead; Cæsar lives: let him live, and take his
brother's place, since fate will have it so.

He rang the bell, caused refreshments to be
brought, and was in excellent spirits.

Francisco was forgotten, and the Pope thought
of nothing else than to open to the daring Cæsar

a wider field in which he might exercise his
dangerous talents. The latter, in the mean time,
crowned the King of Naples, with hands yet reeking with fraternal blood. He returned to Rome;
and Faustus saw, with a malicious laugh, the cardinals and the ambassadors of Spain and Venice
receive the fratricide, whom they knew for such,
at the city-gate, and then conduct him in triumph
to the Pope, who embraced him with great tenderness. Vanosa laid aside her mourning, and
celebrated the day of his return by a festival, at
which appeared all the grandees of Rome. Cæsar
shortly afterwards changed his cardinal's hat for a
helmet, and was with much pomp and magnificence consecrated Gonfalonier, or Standard-bearer
of the Holy See.

The Devil saw, with much pleasure, Faustus
endeavouring, by the wildest excesses, to escape
the pangs by which his heart was now torn. He
remarked how every new scene of horror he was
doomed to witness galled his soul, and that he
was becoming more and more convinced that all
he saw or heard had its origin in the nature of

man. The Devil supported him in this idea by
sophisms, which later philosophers have worked
up into systems. He ransacked the earth of its
treasures, and showered gold and precious gems
upon his victim; and Faustus, dishonouring the
wives and daughters of Rome, believed that he
could not sufficiently corrupt the human family,
which, in his opinion, was doomed to misfortune
and destruction. The lessons he had learnt from
Lucretia had long since poisoned his senses. All
the sweet ties of humanity, which had so long
fettered his heart, were now totally destroyed.
He represented the world to himself as a stormy
sea, on which the human race is cast, and is tossed
here and there by the wind, which drives this man
upon a rock, where he is dashed to pieces, and
blows the other happily to his haven. But what
seemed to Faustus most incomprehensible was,
that the shipwrecked mariner should be punished
in an after-state for not having guided his vessel
better; when the rudder which had been given
him to shape his course by was so weak that any
extraordinary billow could not fail to shatter it.

A new scene now presented itself. Alexander had determined on taking the amusements of the chase at Ostia. He was accompanied thither by a vast throng of cardinals, bishops, ladies, and nuns; the latter being summoned from their cloisters, and, by their beauty, rendering the cavalcade a glorious spectacle. The Devil was constantly by the side of the Pope, and Faustus and Lucretia were inseparable. Every one abandoned himself at Ostia to pleasure, and in the course of a few days excesses were committed there from which even Tiberius and Nero might have learnt something. Faustus had now an excellent opportunity of examining man in his nakedness, as the Devil had expressively termed it; but what were all these scenes of wickedness when compared with the plans which the Pope formed with his bastards, by way of relaxation, in the presence of Faustus and the Devil? It was here determined that Alphonso of Arragon, the husband of Lucretia, should be assassinated, in order that they might give the King of France a proof that they were willing to break entirely with the King of Naples,

R

and to assist the former in his usurpation of the
crown of Sicily.   Louis the Twelfth had already,
with the approbation of Alexander, invaded Italy,
and the Borgias thereby saw all their projects
ripening.   Lucretia intrusted this bloody deed to
the management of her brother, and already considered herself as a widow.   The plan of the
ensuing campaign was then adjusted in a very
expeditious manner; for it was merely to take
possession of all the towns, castles, and domains
of the noblemen of Italy, who were one and all of
them to be murdered, together with their offspring
and relations, in order that not a soul might
remain alive who had the slightest claim upon
the property, and who might therefore trouble
the assassins with future conspiracies.   To support.
the army in the interim, the Pope and Cæsar dic-
tated to Lucretia a list of rich cardinals and prelates, who were to be poisoned successively, and
their goods to be taken possession of by the right
of inheritance vested in the papal chair.

When this secret council was broken up, the
members of it repaired to the grand hall, where

supper awaited them. The Pope was so contented
with his schemes, and the certainty of their accomplishment, that he committed, in his joy, the most
shameful extravagances, and by his example in-
cited his guests to actions similar to what we
have read of in the pages of Petronius Arbiter,
and other, writers of the same character. He,
nevertheless, did not entirely forget the cares of
the state; for he suddenly asked those present
how the revenues of the papal see might be increased, so as to support its numerous army
during the approaching campaign. After various
projects, Ferrara of Modena, Bishop of Patria,
Alexander's worthy minister, by whom he caused
the benefices of the Church to be disposed of to
the highest bidder, proposed that indulgences
should be sold through Europe, under the pretence of an approaching war with the Turks;
adding, like a true papal financier, "that the
foolish idea which men entertained, of being able
to wash away their sins by means of gold, was
the surest source from which the income of a pope
arose."

Lucretia, who lay on the lap of her father, and played with Faustus's yellow locks, incidentally remarked, with a smile,

"The present list of indulgences contains such insipid, antiquated, and absurd crimes, that it is impossible to turn it to much account. It was composed in stupid and barbarous times; and it is now highly necessary to make a new tariff of sin, for which Rome herself can furnish the most important articles."

The company, hot with wine, and reeking from their abominations, eagerly caught up this sally of female wantonness; and the Pope commanded each one present to propose some particular sin, and to tax it; recommending them, above all, to choose those which were most in vogue, and which would consequently bring in the most wealth.

Borgia. Holy father, leave this to the cardinals and prelates; they are better versed in crime than any other people.

Ferrara of Modena sat down to fulfil the office of secretary.

A Cardinal. Absolution to each and every priest who commits fornication, let it be with whom it may; with permission to perform all the duties of the Church, and to receive and hold new benefices, provided he pay into the papal treasury nine gold ducats.

Pope. Write down nine gold ducats, Bishop; and then let us drink absolution to those priests who shall pay the sum.

Each guest filled his glass, and exclaimed in chorus, "Absolutio! dispensatio!"

* * * * *

* * * * *

A Nun. Ha; what means all this? Will no one think of us? Holy father, have we alone no claim to your paternal favour? I entreat you to let us be taxed also, in order that we may sin in peace.

Pope. Right, my daughter; and you shall not be dealt with more hardly than the priests. Bishop, write down: Absolution for each nun who shall commit carnal sin, be it with whom it may, within or out of the circle of the cloister; with full capacity of assuming any conventual dignity when called upon so to do : nine ducats.

Chorus. Absolutio ! dispensatio !

A Bishop. Absolution and dispensation to each priest who publicly keeps a mistress : five ducats.

Lucretia then interposed : " Absolution for carnal knowledge, the enormity of which is indicated by fifteen ducats."

Faustus, whom this scene had horribly mortified, on account of the triumph which it afforded the Devil over him, but who, nevertheless, wished to have a hit at Borgia, exclaimed, with a voice of thunder,

"Absolution to any parricide, matricide, or fratricide, for three ducats."

Pope. Ho, ho, friend ; what are you aiming at now? Will you tax murder lower than fornication ?

Cæsar Borgia. Holy father, he does not wish, by too high a penalty, to deter men from the commission of the crime.

Devil. You are well aware, gentlemen, that the poor are incapable of receiving benefit from any of the above-named absolutions and dispensations.

Chorus (amidst shouts of laughter). Damnation to him who has no money!

Cæsar Borgia. Whoever commits theft, be it sacrilege or not, shall have his soul secured from damnation, upon depositing in the papal treasury three parts of what he has stolen.

Chorus. Absolution to all thieves, sacrilegious or not, provided they share their booty with the Pope.

Pope. Thou hast opened a rich mine, Cæsar. Write that down, Bishop.

Faustus. Absolution to any one who shall practise magic, or enter into an alliance with the Devil. How high shall I tax that, father?

Pope. My son, you will not, by this last article, enrich the papal treasury. The fiend does not understand his own advantage; we call upon him in vain.

Faustus. But provided that should so happen, how high, I repeat?

Pope. For rarity's sake, one hundred ducats.

Faustus. Here they are; and now write me out an absolution, that I may be able to shake it in the face of the Devil, provided I ever sell myself to him.

Chorus. Absolution to him who shall sell himself to the fiend.

A Nun. Most reverend Bishop, since you are writing out the absolution for the magician, be so good as to furnish me with a paper likewise,— you know for what. Here is my rosary; it is worth fifteen ducats; I shall have, therefore, something in bank until another absolution becomes necessary.

Ferrara wrote, and the Pope signed his name beneath.

Devil. Does your holiness imagine that Satan will pay any regard to these scraps of paper?

The grand inquisitor snatched his hand out of the bosom of an abbess, and screamed, with stammering tongue:

"I smell heresy! Who is the atheist? who has uttered that blasphemy?"

The Pope pressed his forefinger softly upon

the mouth of the Devil, and said, "Cavalier, these
are state secrets: handle them not; for if you do,
I myself, with all my authority, shall not be able
to protect you."

Every male in the assembly now opened his
purse, either from a wish to pay his court to the
Pope, or to quiet his conscience. The Bishop had
so many applications, that he was soon obliged to
call in other secretaries, to assist him in expedit-
ing absolutions. Each applicant took away his
particular license, and each sought and found an
opportunity of using it during the remainder of
the night. Never were sins committed with more
quiet minds.

Ferrara of Modena, the next day, caused this
tariff to be fairly copied; he then sent it to the
press,* and caused it to be secretly circulated
throughout Christendom.

Cæsar Borgia did not forget the promise which
he had made to his sister. Alphonso of Arragon
was dispatched on the steps of the Gonfalonier's

* See *Taxæ Cancellariæ Apostolicæ*, &c., printed at Rome
and Paris.

palace, at the moment he was about to enter, in order to be present at a play to which all the nobility of Rome had been invited, and which represented the victories of the great Cæsar, whom Borgia intended henceforward to imitate, if not excel. This latter personage shortly after marched out of Rome with his army; and, within the space of a few months, the Devil purloined from the Pope's pocket the following letter, which he gave Faustus to read:

"REVEREND FATHER,—

"I kiss the feet of your holiness. Victory and fortune have followed my steps, and I drag them behind my car like slaves. I hope now that Cæsar is worthy of his name; for I also can say, *Veni, vidi, vici.* The Duke of Urbino has fallen into the snare which I laid for him. By virtue of your holiness' letter, I asked him for his artillery to fight your enemies with. Dazzled by the marks of friendship and affection which I showed him, and which flattered his self-love, he sent to me a gentleman with his consent in writing. Having thus a very decent pretence, I instantly despatched some thousands of men to Urbino, who, by my commands, took possession of that city and of the whole duchy. The duke, unfortunately, escaped; but I revenged myself for his flight upon the powerful and dangerous family of Montefeltro, and annihilated their whole race. Vitelozzo was fool enough to join me, with all his troops, near Camerino. I deceived Cæsar di Varono by promising him honourable conditions if he would evacuate Camerino, and I attacked the city at the very moment he was engaged in signing the articles of capitulation. I had hoped to have exterminated the whole family at once; but the father found means to elude me. However, I strangled his wife, and cut the throats of his two sons; and I flatter myself that despair and grief will soon send the old fellow after them. I left Camerino, and despatched Paul Orsino, Vitelozzo, and Oliverotto, to Sinegaglia, with orders to take the town by storm, so that they might prepare their future grave with their own hands. When I saw them all in the net, I sent forward my trusty Michelotto and his associates, with directions to seize the fools

when I should give the signal. I then put myself upon the march, and Orsino, Vitelozzo, and
Oliverotto came to meet me, and pay me their
respects. They had left all the troops behind
them, according to my expectations. I received
them with caresses, and went with them into the
city; and at the very moment my people fell
upon their straggling soldiers, Michelotto and his
comrades each seized his man. Thus I made myself master of the domains and fortresses of those
whom we deceived by pretending to assist them
in subduing their enemies. The following night
I caused them to be slaughtered in their dungeons.
Michelotto, to whom I intrusted this business,
told me, with much laughter, that all the mercy
Vitelozzo prayed for was, *that he might not be murdered until he had received, from your holiness, absolution for his sins.* Who now will tell me that it
requires much art to make oneself master of the
minds of men ? As soon as your holiness shall
have put out of the way the Orsinis and the rest,
I will send the Pagolas, the Duke of Gravina, and
my other prisoners, to bear them company. If

Carraccioli, General of the Venetians, whose lovely
wife I seized upon her journey, and who now
sweetens my labour, should come to Rome with
his *complaint*, send him Michelotto's brother to be
his physician. I hear that he is a turbulent, hot-
headed fellow, and therefore it will be as well to
get rid of him. The tumult of arms has not made
me forget my sister's widowhood: the envoy of the
eldest son of the Duke of Este is already on the
way to marry her, in his name. We have now
massacred the most dangerous of our foes; if we
can win over or exterminate (which is almost the
same thing) the houses of Este and Medici, who
will then have the audacity to oppose the Borgias
in Italy? I kiss the feet of your holiness.

"CÆSAR BORGIA, Gonfalonier."

Faustus, after reading this letter, looked angrily upward; but the Devil, without giving
him time to moralise, led him to the Vatican,
where they found the Pope overjoyed at the success which had attended his weapons. He had
already ordered the remaining Orsinis, Alvianis,

Santa Croces, and the other cardinals and archbishops, to be arrested, and awaited the event with impatience. All Rome hastened to congratulate him. Those who were marked out for destruction were seized in the Vatican, conducted into different prisons, and privately executed; whilst the myrmidons of the Pope plundered their palaces. The Cardinal Orsini alone was sent to the Castle of Saint Angelo, and was permitted, for a few days, to be supplied with food from his mother's kitchen; but the Pope, having heard that he possessed a pearl, very precious on account of its extraordinary size, retracted this favour. The mother of the once mighty and flourishing Orsinis went to the Vatican, and offered the Pope the pearl and two thousand crowns if he would liberate her son; when he seized the pearl and the money with one hand, and with the other gave the sign for the cardinal's execution.

When Cæsar Borgia learnt that the Pope had accomplished his design, he instantly commanded all his own prisoners to be assassinated; and, entering Rome in triumph, shared, with his holi-

. ness and the other illegitimates, the booty he had brought with him; and, in return, received his dividend of the confiscated property of the slaughtered cardinals and ecclesiastics.

The marriage of Lucretia was soon afterwards celebrated with more than Asiatic pomp, and the Romans contributed to render it as brilliant as possible. The bells pealed from the churches; the artillery thundered from Saint Angelo; there were bull-fights; the most immoral and indecent comedies were performed; and the delighted populace shouted before the Vatican, "Long live Pope Alexander! long live Lucretia, Duchess of Este!" Faustus huzzaed with the best of them, and said to the Devil: "If these acclamations ascend to heaven with the groans of the assassinated, which will the Eternal believe?" The fiend bowed himself to the earth, and was silent.

In order to crown the festivities of the marriage, Alexander and his daughter commanded a spectacle which must for ever stand unparalleled in the annals of human infamy. The Pope sat, with his daughter, upon a couch, in a vast il-

luminated hall. Faustus, the Devil, and others
who had been invited to this scene, stood around
them. Suddenly the doors opened, and in rushed
fifty nude courtesans,—more beautiful than the
houris in Mahomet's paradise,—and performed, to
the voluptuous sound of flutes and other instruments, a dance which decency forbids us to de-
scribe, although it was a Pope who designed the
figure. When the dance was ended, his Holiness
gave the signal for a combat which we are still
less permitted to depict,—he himself holding the
prize of victory. They proclaimed Faustus to be
the conqueror. Lucretia overwhelmed him with
kisses, and crowned him with laurels ; while the
Pope delivered to him the prize,—a golden goblet,
on which Lucretia had caused to be engraven
the School of Pleasure. Faustus gave it the
very next day to a Venetian monk, in whose
possession Aretino saw it a long time afterwards, and illustrated some of its incidents in
his sonnets.

The Pope, on the day of his daughter's marriage, had made an election of cardinals, choosing

only the richest prelates for that dignity. Cæsar
Borgia, being in want of large sums of money for
the next campaign, determined to send some of
the newly-elected into the other world, at a festival which his father intended to give at one of
his villas. [The details of these marriage-fes-
tivities are omitted; inasmuch as the grossness
of the spectacle renders it unfit for the general
reader. The conduct of Lucretia Borgia has been
the subject of much obloquy, which her defenders
maintain rests chiefly on inferences from her living
in a flagitious court, where she witnessed the most
profligate scenes. It is asserted that some of the
accusations have no better foundation than the •
epigrams of Pontano, and other Neapolitan poets,
the natural enemies of her family.—*Transl.*] The
Pope went in a coach, with his daughter, the
Devil, Faustus, Borgia, and the wife of the Venetian general. Here, after witnessing a gross spectacle, Lucretia retired with Faustus; and Borgia
went with the Venetian; and the Pope remained
alone with the Devil. His holiness now made to
the fiend certain proposals, which so exasperated

the Devil that he appeared under a form which no mortal eye had ever yet been able to sustain. The Pope, who knew him immediately, uttered a cry of joy.

"Ah, ben venuto Signor Diavolo! You could not have come to me at a more seasonable time than the present; I have long wished to see you, for I know perfectly well what a deal of use might be made of so powerful a spirit as yourself. Ha, ha, ha! you please me now much better than you did before, you rogue, you! Come, be my friend; assume your former figure, and I will make you a cardinal; for you only can raise me at once to the height which I wish to attain. I entreat you to destroy my foes, procure me money, and drive the French out of Italy, since I have no further occasion for them. This to you will merely be the work of a moment; and you may then ask me for any reward you please. But by all means do not discover yourself to my son Cæsar: he is so great a wretch, that I verily believe he would poison me, his father, in order to become, by thy help, King of Italy and Pope at the same time."

The Devil, who had at first been a little mortified that his frightful exterior had produced no greater effect, was now unable to refrain from laughing; for what he saw and heard surpassed every thing which had as yet come to the knowledge of hell. But recovering himself, he said, with a serious air,

"Pope Alexander, Satan once showed to the Son of the Eternal all the kingdoms of the world, and offered him them, if he would fall down and worship him."

Pope. I understand you. He was a God, and wanted nothing; had he been a man, and a pope, he would have done what I will now do.

He fell upon his knees, and kissed the fiend's feet.

The Devil stamped upon the floor, so that the whole villa trembled. Faustus and Lucretia, Cæsar and the Venetian, saw through the door, which had been burst open by the shock, the Pope kneeling with clasped hands before the frightful figure of the Devil, who seized the trembling miscreant, strangled him, and gave his soul to an attendant spirit to be conveyed to hell. Borgia fell to the ground in an agony of terror; and the horrible spectacle brought upon him an illness, which soon sent him after his father. The body of the Pope, frightfully disfigured, was buried with much pomp; and his historians, who are not well acquainted with his tragic end, invented the story, which is partly founded on truth, that he and his son having drunk, by the cupbearer's mistake, some poisoned wine which had been intended for the cardinals, were thus caught in their own net.

CHAPTER V.

THE horrible death of the Pope, and the frightful figure of the Devil, whom Faustus had hitherto
only seen majestic and comely, made so strong
an impression upon him, that he hastened from
the villa to Rome; and, having packed up his
things, instantly departed, with perturbed mind
and beating heart. His spirit had become so
weak from all that he had seen and heard, that
he who once dared to defy the Eternal in thought
scarcely ventured now to look Satan in the face,
though he still had absolute dominion over him.
Hatred and contempt for men, cruel doubt, in-
difference to every thing which occurred around
him, murmurings at the insufficiency of his moral
and physical powers, were the rewards of his experience and the fruits of his life; yet he consoled
himself with the idea that what he had witnessed

authorised in him these gloomy sentiments, and
confirmed him in the opinion, that there either
existed on earth no connexion between man and
his Creator, or that, if any did exist, such connexion ran so confusedly and equivocally through
the labyrinth of life, that it was impossible for
the eye of man to follow it. He yet flattered
himself with the delusion, that his crimes, when
added to the vast mass of earthly wickedness,
would be like a drop of water falling into the
ocean. The Devil willingly permitted him to
repose in this dream, in order that the blow he
intended for him might fall with greater violence.
Faustus resembled those men of the world who
abandon themselves to their pleasures without
thinking of the consequences; and at length,
worn out and dejected, look morosely on the
world, and judge of the human race according to
their own sad experience, without reflecting that
they have only trodden the worst paths of life,
and seen the worst part of the creation. In a
word, he was on the point of becoming a philosopher of the species of Voltaire, who, whenever

he found the *bad*, always held it forth to public view ; and, with unexampled industry, always endeavoured to keep the *good* in the background.

Faustus was lying in a sweet morning slumber on the frontiers of Italy, when a portentous dream depicted itself to his soul in the liveliest colours ; and this dream was followed by a frightful apparition. He saw the Genius of Man, whom he had once before seen. He saw him upon a vast and blooming island, surrounded by a stormy sea, wandering up and down, and looking very anxiously upon the raging billows. The ocean was covered with innumerable barks, in which men, aged and young, children, women, and maidens, of all the nations of the world, were struggling against the tempest, in order to reach the island. When they arrived there, their first care was to bring to land different building materials, which they flung together confusedly. After an immense number had gained the shore, the Genius marked out, upon the most elevated part of the island, the plan of a vast edifice; and each of the crowd, young and old, weak or strong, took, according to his or her strength, a piece from the mass of materials, and, directed by those whom the Genius had chosen, carried it, and deposited it at the proper place. All worked with pleasure, with courage, and without relaxation; and the fabric had already risen high above the ground, when they were suddenly attacked by numerous foes, who advanced out of a dark ambush in three columns. At the head of each of these columns stood a general. The first bore a glittering crown upon his head; on his brazen shield was written the word *Power;* and in his right hand he held a sceptre, which, like the rod of Mercury, had a snake and a scourge twisted round it. Before him went a fierce hyena, holding in its jaws a book, on the back of which was written *My Word.* His troops were armed with swords, spears, and other implements of destruction. The second column was commanded by a majestic matron, whose noble figure was clothed in a sacerdotal robe. On her right stood *Superstition,* a gloomy-eyed spectre, bearing in his hand a bow formed from the bones of the dead, and on his back a quiver filled with poisoned arrows. On her left hovered a wild, fantastically clothed figure, called *Fanaticism*, bearing a blazing torch. These two phantoms, with menacing gestures and frightful grimaces, led the noble matron in chains, like a prisoner. Before them went *Ambition*, whose head was adorned with a triple crown; in his hand was an episcopal staff, and on his mailed breast shone the word *Religion*. Fanaticism and Superstition waited, with the utmost impatience, until Religion should give them the signal to vent their fury, which they could scarcely restrain. The army was a confused and howling rabble, and each soldier carried a dagger and a flaming torch. The chief of the third column advanced with bold and haughty steps; he was clothed in the simple dress of the sages, and was called *Philosophy*. He bore in his hand, as did all his followers, a golden cup, filled with foaming and intoxicating liquor. These two last armies howled and screamed so frightfully, that even the bellowing of the waters and the roar of the tempest were no longer audible.

When the three columns arrived near the
labourers, they united, by the directions of their
generals, and attacked them furiously with their
murderous weapons. The most courageous of the
workmen flung away their implements of labour,
and drew their swords, which hung at their belts,
in order to drive their foes back. The others, in
the mean time, endeavoured, with redoubled zeal,
to complete the fabric they had begun. The
Genius protected his brave warriors and his industrious labourers with a huge glittering shield,
which was handed to him from the sky; but he
could not cover the whole of the countless multitude. He saw with deep sorrow thousands of his
people sink to the earth beneath the swords and
poisoned darts of their adversaries. Many allowed
themselves to be ensnared by the invitations and
allurements of those who offered them the enchanted cup to refresh themselves with; and, in
their intoxication, they soon destroyed the laborious work of their hands.

Those who bore torches made their way with
their daggers, and hurled the torches into the

unfinished edifice, when the flames, rearing up,
threatened to reduce it to ashes. The Genius
looked mournfully upon the slain, and on those
who had been intoxicated by the deceitful bever-
age; but he encouraged the rest, and inspired
them, by his firmness and his dignity, with
strength and patience. They extinguished the
flames; replaced what the others had overturned;
and laboured, amid death and destruction, with
so much zeal, that, in spite of the fury and
malignity of their foes, they raised at length
a vast and sublime temple. The Genius then
healed the wounded, comforted the weary, praised
the bold warriors, and conducted them all, amid
songs of triumph, into the temple. The foes
stood confounded at the enormous work; and,
after they had in vain attempted to shatter its
solidity, they retreated, with rage in their hearts.
Faustus now found himself upon the island. The
field around the majestic building was covered
with dead bodies of all ages and of both sexes; and
those who had tasted of the enchanted cup walked
coolly among the corpses, disputed with each other,

and laughed at and criticised the structure of
the temple. Faustus went past them, and as he
approached the edifice he read over the entrance
the following words: "Mortal, if thou hast bravely
struggled, and hast remained faithful, enter, and
learn to know thy noble destiny."

At these words he felt his heart leap with joy,
and he hoped to be now able to penetrate the
obscurity which had so long tormented him.
With bold and daring pace he ran up the lofty
steps, and caught a glimpse of the interior of
the edifice, which seemed filled with the roseate
colours of morning. He heard the soft voice of
the Genius, and was about to enter; but the gate
of brass closed before him with a harsh sound,
and he recoiled in terror. His desire to penetrate
into the secrets of the temple was increased by
the impossibility. All of a sudden he felt wings,
and rising high into the air, he precipitated
himself furiously against the brazen gate, was
hurled back, and started out of his sleep just as
he was on the point of touching the ground.
He opened his eyes in dismay. A ghastly figure,

wrapped in a winding-sheet, drew back the cur-
tains of his bed. He recognised the features of
his old father, who, gazing upon him for a moment, said, in a lamentable voice:

"Faustus! Faustus! never yet did father beget a more unfortunate son; and in this feeling I
have just died. For ever—ah! for ever!—must
the gulf of damnation lie between thee and me."

The portentous dream and this horrible apparition filled the soul of Faustus with affright.
He sprang from his bed, and opened the window
to inhale the fresh air. Before him lay the enormous Alps, whose tops were just gilded by the
rising sun. He surveyed them for some time,
and at last fell into a profound reverie. He trembled as he thought of his nocturnal vision, and
was endeavouring to explain to himself its most
prominent passages, when, falling anew into his
cruel doubts, he exclaimed:

"Whence came those monsters who attacked
the industrious labourers? By whom were they
authorised to disturb and destroy them while engaged in their noble occupation? Who permitted

it? Was he who permitted it unable, or did
he not wish, to hinder it? And why did the
Supreme Genius protect and save only a part
of them who were assailed by those cannibals?
Were some predestined to perish, in order that
the others might triumph and taste repose? Who,
then, will dare to tell me that I am not one of
those who are born with destruction for their lot?
What evil had those unfortunates committed,
and why should those be esteemed criminal who,
pressed by a burning thirst, endeavoured to quench
it by tasting the enchanted cup?"

Faustus wandered for a long time in a maze
of doubt; but, remembering the apparition of his
father, it brought back to his mind his long-
forgotten family. He instantly determined to
return to them; to become again a member of
society; to resume his business; and to get rid of
his infernal companion. He pursued his journey
towards home like many others, who, mistaking
the ardour of insensate youth for genius, enter
upon the career of the world with high pretensions, and, having quickly exhausted the little fire

which their souls possess, soon find themselves a
burden to their kindred and their friends, at the
very place from whence they started. Faustus
brooded over all this, while he rode silently and
moodily by the side of the Devil.

The latter left him to his reflections, laughed
inwardly at his resolution, and shortened the time
with the sweet idea of soon being able to breathe
the pleasant vapours of hell. He determined to
have a bitter laugh at Satan, who had represented
to him as a man of superior strength of mind this
Faustus, whom he now saw completely dejected
even before he knew the horrors of his fate, He
compared his present downcast and timid looks
with the haughty and bold glances he had cast
upon him when he first made him appear before
his magic circle. His hatred against him increased, and he rejoiced in his black soul when he
saw Worms lie before them in the plain.

They rode towards the celebrated city; and
when they were about half a mile distant from it,
they perceived a gibbet, to which was suspended
a tall, slender youth. Faustus lifted up his eyes

and gazed upon him. The evening wind blew freshly among his long hair, which half-concealed his face, and swung his body to and fro. Faustus burst into tears at this spectacle, and cried, with trembling voice :

" Poor youth! hanging at the cursed tree before thou hadst reached the flower of life ! What sin hast thou committed, which induced the tribunal of men to cut thee off so soon ?"

Devil (in a solemn and impressive tone). Faustus, this is thy work.

Faustus. My work !

Devil. Thy work. Look at him closer. He is thy eldest son.

Faustus looked up, recognised him, and sunk from his horse.

Devil. Cry and groan! The hour approaches in which I must remove the thick veil from before thine eyes, and blow away, with a single breath, the labyrinth in which thou hast so long wandered. I will fling light upon the moral world, and show thee how thou hast outraged it by each of thy actions. I, a devil, will show thee what

are the consequences when a worm like thyself
dares to stop the wheel of so exact and so enormous a machine. Dost thou remember the youth
whom I, at our departure from Mayence, saved
from drowning by thy command? I gave thee
warning, but thou wouldst obey the rash impulse
of thy heart. If thou hadst permitted that miscreant to perish, thy son would not now be rotting
on yon gibbet. He on whose account thou didst
change the order of things, insinuated himself,
shortly after thy departure, into the society of thy
young wife. The glitter of the gold which we
had left her in such abundance, attracted him
much more than her youth and beauty. It was no
difficult thing for him to win the affections of her
who had been forsaken by thee; and in a short
time he gained such influence over her, that she
delivered up herself and all she possessed to his
will and control. Thy old father endeavoured to
oppose his shameless sway; but the young man
insulted him and beat him: the poor old man
sought an asylum in the workhouse, where he died,
a few days ago, of grief for thee and thy family.

T

Thy son, having taken his grandfather's part, and threatened the life of his mother's seducer, was by him turned out of the house also. The boy wandered among the woods and wildernesses till he was half famished. Arriving at length in this city, and being ashamed to beg, he stole a few pence from the poor-box in a church, in order to assuage his hunger; but he committed this theft so artlessly, that several people perceived him, and the most worshipful magistrate, in consideration of his youth, sentenced him only to be hanged: he was accordingly hanged; although he protested, with tears, that for the last four days he had swallowed nothing but grass. Thy daughter is at Frankfort, where she subsists upon the earnings of vice; thy second son is in the profligate service of an infamous prelate. The young man whom thou didst save from death robbed thy wife not long ago of her last stiver; thy friend whom we preserved from beggary refused thy old father the slightest assistance, and spurned thy children from his door when they came to him for bread. And I will now show thee thy family, in order that thou mayest see to what a state thou hast reduced them. I will then bring thee here again, and hold reckoning with thee; for I am no longer thy slave—thou art mine. The worm of despair begins to gnaw within thee; thou art no longer fit to live, and hell only is fit to receive thee.

The Devil seized the wretched man, flew with him to Mayence, and showed him his wife and two youngest children sitting at the gate of the Franciscan convent in expectation of the remnant of the monks' supper. When the mother beheld Faustus, she screamed, "O Heaven! Faustus! your father—" then, covering her eyes with her hands, she fell into a swoon. The children ran to him, clung about him, and cried for bread.

Faustus. Devil, decide upon my fate: let it be more frightful than the heart of man can support or conceive, but supply these unfortunate crea-tures with bread, and rescue them from misery and hunger.

Devil. I have plundered for thee the earth of its treasures; thou hast sacrificed them to thy

infamous pleasures, without once thinking of these
wretches. Feel now thy folly; thou hast spun
the web of their destiny, and thy hungry, beg-
garly, miserable brood will transmit to their remotest posterity the misery of which thou art the
cause. Thou didst beget children—wherefore hast
thou not been a father to them? Wherefore hast
thou sought happiness where mortal never yet
found it? Look at them once more. In hell
thou shalt see them again; and they will there
curse thee for the inheritance which thou didst
entail upon them.

He tore him from his miserable family at the
moment the wife was about to embrace his knees,
and to ask his pardon. Faustus wished to comfort her; but the Devil grasped him, and placed
him once more beneath the gibbet at Worms.

Night sunk dark upon the earth. Faustus
stood gazing on the remains of his unfortunate
son; madness glowed in his brain, and he cried,
in the wild tone of despair:

"Devil, let me bury this poor victim; take
then my life, and bear me to hell, where I shall

never again see men in flesh and bone. I have learnt to know them; I am disgusted with them, with their destination, with the world, and with life. Since one good action brings on my head such inexpressible evils, I have reason to believe that the wicked only have a right to happiness. If such be the order of things in this world, hurl me at once into hell. Its darkness is a thousand times preferable to the light of day.

Devil. Not so fast, Faustus. In the first place, I take away from thee thy mighty magic rod, and confine thee in the narrow circle which I draw around thee. Here shalt thou listen to me, and howl and tremble. I will unfold to thee the consequences of thy deeds, and will assassinate thee through downright despair.

"Fool! thou sayest thou hast learnt to know man! Where? How and when hast thou attained this knowledge? Hast thou ever sounded his nature? Hast thou separated from him that which he has acquired, and which is foreign to him? Hast thou distinguished that which proceeds from his heart, from that which is merely

the effect of an imagination corrupted by artifice?
Hast thou compared the wants and the desires
resulting from his nature, with those which he
owes to civilisation? Hast thou considered man
in his proper shape, where each of his move-
ments bears the stamp of his inward disposition?
*Thou hast taken the mask of society for his natural
figure; and thou hast only known that man whom
his titles, his rank, his riches, his power, and his
acquirements have corrupted. Thou hast only known
him who has sacrificed his nature to thy own idol,—
to vanity.* Thou hast merely frequented palaces
and courts, where men spurn away the unfortunate, and laugh at the complaints of the oppressed, whilst they are dissipating in revel-rout
and roar that which they have robbed them of.
Thou hast seen the sovereigns of the world; thou
hast seen tyrants surrounded by their parasites
and their infamous courtesans; and thou hast
seen priests who make use of religion as an instrument of oppression. Such are the men thou hast
seen, and not him who groans under the heavy
yoke, and comforts himself with the hope of

futurity. Thou hast passed by with disdain the hut of the poor and simple man, who does not even know your artificial wants by name, who gains his bread by the sweat of his brow, shares it faithfully with his wife and children, and rejoices, at the last moment of his life, in having completed his long and laborious task. If thou hadst opened his door, thou wouldst not indeed have found a vain ideal of heroic and over-refined virtue, which is only the offspring of your vices and your crimes; but thou wouldst have seen a man who, in meekness and resigned magnanimity, shows more force of soul, than do your renowned heroes in their blood-stained fields of battle, or your ministers in their perfidious cabinets. If it were not for these, and for your priests, and above all for your false philosophers, the gates of hell would soon be closed. Canst thou say that thou knowest man, when thou hast only sought for him in the paths of vice and crime? Dost thou know thyself? I will make your wounds yet deeper, and pour poison into them. But if I had a thousand human tongues, and were to keep thee here

confined for as many years, I should still be unable to enumerate to thee all the frightful consequences of thy actions and thy temerity. Know
now the result of thy life, and remember, that I
have scarcely fulfilled one of thy insensate desires
without having forewarned thee to check it. It
is by thy command that I have interrupted the
course of things, and committed crimes which I
myself could scarcely have imagined; so that,
devil as I am, I am not so bad as thyself.

"Dost thou remember the nun Clara, and the
voluptuous night which thou didst pass with her?
But how canst thou have forgotten her? Listen
now to the consequences. A short time after thy
departure, the Bishop, who was her friend and
protector, died; and she, having become a mother,
was condemned, as an object of public horror, to
be starved with her child in a dark dungeon. In
her ravenous hunger she fell upon the newly-
born, ate of thy flesh and her own, and prolonged
her existence as long as there was a bone for her
to gnaw. In what had she sinned?—she who did
not comprehend her crime; she who did not know,

or even suspect, the author of her ignominy and her frightful death. Feel now the result of one single moment of pleasure, and tremble! Hast thou not strengthened the delusion which condemned her? Must not hell now bear the reproach of thy crime? Those people condemned the child as the spawn of Satan, and murdered the mother under the idea that she had been possessed by him; and through this thy deed thou hast bewildered their minds, and those of their posterity.

"Thou wast not more fortunate with the Prince Bishop. He caused, it is true, Hans Ruprecht to be buried, and provided for his family. He likewise, by the trick I played him, lost his fat, and became the most mild and merciful of princes; but he so relaxed the band of social order by his over-indulgence, that his subjects soon became a horde of drunkards, sluggards, ruffians, and highwaymen. The present Bishop is obliged to be their executioner, and to disperse and destroy a hundred families, in order that the rest, terrified by their example, may again become humanised, and submit to the laws. The furies themselves could not do half the injury to these people which those now do to whom the Bishop has been obliged to intrust the sword of justice and the power of vengeance.

"Doctor Robertus, the renowned champion of freedom, the man after thine own heart, was from his earliest youth an enemy to the Minister, whom he hated on account of his talents. Envy and jealousy caused his independence of spirit; and if he had been in the situation of the other, he would have adopted with pleasure the most cruel principles of despotism, for which his wild and ferocious heart was only formed. The honest man was the Minister; Robertus was a monster, who would have set the whole world in a blaze, and has done it partly, in order to satisfy his boundless ambition. Thou didst oblige me to rescue him, and to furnish him with a large sum of money. He made such good use of his freedom, his gold, and the enthusiasm which his miraculous escape had caused among the people, that he soon succeeded in stirring up a dreadful rebellion. He

armed the peasants; they murdered the nobility,
and desolated the whole land. The noble Minister fell a victim to his revenge; and Robertus, the
friend of liberty, the champion of the oppressed, is
the author of the calamitous war of the peasants,
which by degrees will spread over the whole of
Germany, and will ravage it. Murders, assassi-
nations, robberies, and sacrilege are now committed with impunity; and thy noble hero stands
at the head of a furious rabble, and threatens to
make Germany the cemetery of the human race.
Satan himself could not have laboured more
effectually for the destruction of mankind, than
thou didst when I was forced by thee to rescue
this madman from the stroke of justice.

"Let us now return to the court of the German prince, where thou so audaciously didst make
thyself the avenger of virtue and oppressed innocence. That prince and his favourite affected
virtues which they did not possess; but their
actions contributed to the good of the people,
because both had sense enough to perceive that
the happiness of the people constitutes that of the

prince. Does the thirsty traveller know, or does he care, if the spring of which he drinks gushes out of a mountain filled with poison, provided he cools his hot blood without receiving any harm? That hypocrite displeased thee because he did not answer to thy preconceived high opinion, which thou, for certain reasons, didst wish to thrust upon me; and I was compelled to strangle him by thy orders. His infant son was destined to succeed him in the government. His tutors harassed and oppressed the people, once happy under the dominion of his father; they corrupted the heart and the mind of the future regent, who having enervated his body through early pleasure, they rule him now he is come of age, and are his and his people's tyrants. Hadst thou not compelled me to murder the father, he would have brought up his son in his own maxims; he would have developed his faculties, and have made him a man fit to govern a nation. The numerous subjects who are now groaning beneath iron-handed oppression, and whose misery is all to be imputed to thee, would then have been the happiest in Germany.

Let their tears, their despair, and the horrors of an approaching insurrection, reward thee for having rashly exercised the duty of a judge.

"Madman! in obedience to thy comand, I burnt the castle of the fierce Wildgrave, with all its inhabitants, with his wife and his infant. What crime had they committed? It was a moment of delight to me. If the infant was consumed on the breast of the mother, it was thy work. If the Wildgrave attacked a neighbouring nobleman as the cause of the conflagration, set fire to his house, and ignominiously whipped him, it was thy work. Thousands have already fallen beneath their reciprocal vengeance, and tranquillity will not be restored to that part of Germany until the hostile families shall be completely exhausted and annihilated. And thus, poor worm, hast thou avenged the innocent; thou, who all thy life hast been wallowing in the grossest sensuality; thou, who didst pull me out of hell merely to satiate thy lusts. Groan and weep; but I will overwhelm thee with fresh horrors.

"By thy order I infused the poison of lust

into the heart of the innocent Angelica, she who
was the ornament of her sex and of the world.
Thou didst enjoy her in the wild intoxication of
thy senses, and she scarcely knew what had happened to her. Shudder at the consequences! I,
who find pleasure in evil and destruction, think
with pity and compassion on her end. She fled
from her native place, and a feeling of shame
forced her to conceal the state in which she found
herself, and to which thou hadst reduced her.
Alone, in solitude, and without help, amid ago-
nising throes and deadly pains, she became a
mother. The child died as soon as it saw the
light of day. She, the wretched victim of thy
momentary pleasure, was cast into prison, and
publicly executed as an infanticide. Thou shouldst
have seen her in the last moments of her life;
thou shouldst have seen her pure blood spouting
high into the air, when the sword of the executioner separated her lovely neck."

Faustus gave a loud groan. Despair was raging in his heart.

Devil. The daughter of the miser in France,

whom thou didst seduce, and in whose bosom thou didst cause slumbering desire to awake, became shortly afterwards the mistress of the youthful king. She ruled him entirely, and in order that he might not disturb her in her intercourse with another lover, she urged him to the disastrous expedition into Italy, and brought misfortunes upon France which many future reigns will not be able to heal. The flower of the French nobility, and the heroes of the kingdom, are rotting on the sun-scorched plains of Italy; and the king has returned home overwhelmed with shame and ignominy. Thus, wherever thou hast wandered, thou hast scattered around thee the seeds of misery, which have sprung up, and will bear fruit to all eternity.

"Thou didst not pay attention to the look I gave thee when I tore down the house upon the cruel physicians at Paris. I had previously told thee that, by my destructive hand, thou didst mangle the moral world worse than they did the flesh of their fellow-creatures. Thou didst pay no attention to that look—hear now the cause of

it. Those wretches deserve to perish beneath the
ruins of their laboratory; but what evil had the
poor people committed who lodged in the lower
part of the house, and who were totally ignorant
of what was going forward above their heads?
Why should an innocent, happy family be crushed
along with those monsters? To satisfy thy blind
vengeance, I was forced to bury them beneath
stones and falling timbers. Judge and avenger
at the same time, thou hadst not thought of this.
Consider now all the consequences of thy delirium
and thy folly; cast thine eyes along the whole
chain, extending to the remotest posterity, and
then sink beneath the terrible survey. Did I not
once tell thee that man is much more rash in his
decisions and in his vengeance, than the Devil is
in the accomplishment of wickedness?"

Faustus opened his haggard eyes, and looked
towards heaven.

Devil. It is deaf to thee. Be proud of having lived a moment when thy atrocity was so
great that it almost made the deeds of the devils
themselves forgotten. I speak of that moment

when thou didst command me to withdraw the veil which concealed the Eternal from thy sight. The angel whose charge it was to register thy sins averted his face, and struck thy name from the Book of Life.

Faustus (springing up). Cursed be thou; cursed be myself; cursed be the hour of my birth; cursed be he who begot me; cursed be the breast which I sucked!

Devil. O the delightful moment! Precious reward of my toils! Hell rejoices at thy curses, and expects a yet more frightful one from thee. Fool! wast thou not born free? Didst thou not bear in thy breast, like all who live in flesh, the instinct of good as well as of evil? Why didst thou transgress, with so much temerity, the bounds which had been prescribed to thee? Why didst thou endeavour to try thy strength with and against Him who is not to be reached? Did not God create you in such a manner, that you were as much elevated above the devils as above the beasts of the earth? Did he not grant you the perceptive faculty of good and evil? Were

U

not your will and choice free? We wretches are
without choice, without will; we are the slaves of
evil and of imperious necessity; constrained and
condemned to all eternity to wish nothing but
evil, we are the instruments of revenge and punishment upon you. Ye are kings of the creation,
free beings, masters of your destiny, which ye fix
yourselves; masters of the future, which only
depends upon your actions. It is on account of
these prerogatives that we detest you, and rejoice
when, by your follies, your impatience, and your
crimes, you cease to be masters of yourselves. It
is only in resignation, Faustus, that present or
future happiness consists. Hadst thou remained
what thou wast, and had not doubt, pride, vanity,
and voluptuousness torn thee out of the happy
and limited sphere for which thou wast born, thou
mightst have followed an honourable employment,
and have supported thy wife and children; and
thy family, which is now sunk into the refuse of
humanity, would have been blooming and prosperous; lamented by them, thou wouldst have
died calmly on thy bed, and thy example would

have guided thy posterity along the thorny path of life.

Faustus. Ah, the greatest torment of the damned is, no doubt, to hear the devil preach penitence.

Devil. It is pleasant enough that you force us to moralise; but, wretch, if the voice of truth and of penitence were to echo down from heaven, you would close your ears to it.

Faustus. Destroy me at once, and do not kill me by thy prattling, which tears my heart without convincing my spirit. Pour out thy venom, and do not distil it upon me drop by drop. I am not to blame if, having sown the seeds of good, bad has arisen from them. A good action has caused the ignominious death of my son, and a good action has precipitated my family into the most profound misery.

Devil. Why dost thou boast to me of thy good deed? How does it deserve that name? I suppose because thou didst give me a command, which, by the by, did not cost thee much. To have made the action meritorious, thou shouldst have cast thyself into the water, and have saved the young man at the risk of thine own life. I brought him to the shore, and disappeared; he would have known thee, and, moved by gratitude, would probably have become the protector, instead of the destroyer, of thy family.

Faustus. Thou canst torment me, Devil; but thou canst not, from stupidity, or thou wilt not, from wickedness, dispel my doubts. Never have they torn my heart more venomously than at this moment, when I consider the miseries of my existence and of my after-destination. Is human life any thing else than a tissue of crimes, torments, pains, hypocrisy, contradictions, and false virtues? What are free agency, choice, will, and that so much vaunted faculty of distinguishing good from evil, if the passions drown the feeble voice of reason, as the roar of the sea drowns the voice of the pilot whose vessel is about to be dashed against the rocks? Is it possible for man to destroy and root out of his breast the germ of evil which has been designedly introduced there? I hate, more bitterly than ever, the' world, my

fellow-creatures, and myself. Destined to suffer,
why was I born with the desire of being happy?
Born for darkness, why was I filled with the desire of seeing light? Why had the slave the
thirst for freedom? Why had the worm the wish
to fly? Why had I a boundless imagination, the
teeming mother of bold desires, daring wishes and
thoughts? Tear from my uncertain and doubtful
soul the flesh which envelops it; destroy in it all
remembrance of its ever having animated a human
body: I wish to become henceforward one of you,
and only to live in the desire of evil. Ah, Devil,
this is not so pleasant to thy ears as the hissing,
howling song of despair which thou didst expect.
But loosen the enchantment which fetters me in
this circle; and let me perform my last sad duty.
I will not attempt to escape from thee; if I could,
I would not, for the pain of hell cannot be greater
than that which I now feel.

Devil. Faustus, I am pleased with thy courage,
and I would sooner hear what thou hast said than
the wild shriek of despair. Be proud that the
force of thy spirit has carried thee even to mad-

ness and blasphemy, for which the pain of hell awaits thee. Step out of thy circle; bury that wretched youth; thy part will then be played here, and thou must begin another, which will never end.

Faustus climbed the gibbet, and cut the rope from the neck of his son. He then bore him into a neighbouring field which the plough had lately turned up, and scratching a grave with his hands, he buried the body of the unfortunate youth. He then returned to the Devil, and said, in a wild tone:

"The measure of my wretchedness is full; break now the vase which can hold nothing more; but I have yet courage to struggle with thee for my life. I will not perish like the slave who yields without resistance to the might of his master. Appear to me under whatever form thou wilt, and I will grapple with thee. For freedom, for independence, I once drew thee out of hell; on its verge I will yet assert my right to both; on the verge of the frightful gulf I will use my strength, and remember that I once saw thee

tremble before my magic circle, when I threatened
to scourge thee with my rod. The tears which
thou seest in my eyes are tears of indignation, of
hate, and of disgust. Not the fiend, but my own
heart, triumphs over me.

Devil. Insipid braggart! With this form I
tear off the mask which belied my courage. Vengeance is at hand, and Leviathan is himself once
more!

He stood in gigantic stature before him. His
eyes glowed like full-laden thunder-clouds, which
reflect the rays of the descending sun. The noise
of his breath was like the rushing of the tempest-
blast. The earth groaned beneath his iron feet.
The storm rustled in his hair, which waved round
his head like the tail from the threatening comet.
Faustus lay before him like a worm; for the horrible sight had deprived him of his senses and
his strength. The Devil uttered a contemptuous
laugh, which hissed over the surface of the earth;
and seizing the trembling being, he tore him to
pieces, as a capricious boy would tear an insect.
He strewed the bloody members with fury and

disgust about the field, and plunged with the soul into the depths of hell.

The devils were assembled round Satan, who was consulting with his princes concerning the punishments which should be inflicted upon Pope Alexander the Sixth. His crimes, and the last moments of his life, had been unparalleled, so that even the worst devils found themselves at a loss to allot him a punishment suitable to his deserts. The Pope stood before his judges, who treated him as contemptuously as a tribunal of princes treats an accused person who has nothing else to recommend him than his being a man. All of a sudden Leviathan rushed triumphantly into the midst, held the soul of Faustus on high, and then hurled it with violence upon the table, saying:

" There you have Faustus !"

He was received with so loud a bellow of joy, that the damned trembled in their pools : " Welcome, Prince Leviathan ! There is Faustus ! There is Faustus !"

Satan. Welcome, prince of hell. Welcome, Faustus ; we have heard enough of you here.

Leviathan. There he is, Satan; see him yourself. He has plagued me not a little, but he has been a good recruit for us, and I hope that thou art contented with my long sojourn upon earth. But I entreat thee, for many centuries to come, to send me no more on such errands; for I am quite weary of the human race. I must, however, acknowledge that this fellow did not badly support the last hour of his life, hard as it was; but that arose, I suppose, from his having applied himself in his youth to that philosophy which thou hast taught mankind.

Satan. I thank thee, Prince Leviathan; and I promise thee that thou shalt long continue with me among the sweet vapours of this place, and scourge the shades of the great princes of the earth for thy pastime. Hem! a fine fellow, and seems to have had quite enough of men and things. Despair, audacity, hate, rancour, agony, and pride, have torn deep furrows in his soul. He looks even at us and hell without trembling. Faustus, art thou become dumb of a sudden?

Faustus. Not from fear, I assure thee. I have

been bold to one much mightier than thyself, and therefore am I here.

Satan. Hey! carry the saucy hound to the pool of the damned; and after being soused therein, let him be well scourged by a legion of my most active pages, in order that he may become a little acquainted with the rules of these regions.

A devil dragged Faustus to the pool; the legion swarmed after him.

Leviathan (perceiving the Pope). Ah! welcome, Pope Alexander. I hope you no longer feel any desire to make a Ganymede of the Devil.

Pope (sighing). No, alas!

Satan. Ha, ha, ha! This is now a good specimen of the men who at present ravage the earth; but let them once get to the new world, and they will make it a theatre of crimes which will put the old one to shame.

Pope. Would that I could be there too!

Satan. A wish truly worthy of a pope; but console thyself,—thy countrymen will murder millions of men for their gold.

Pope. What will men not do for gold?

Faustus came back with his fiendish attendants.

Satan. Well, Faustus, how do you like your bath, and those that rubbed you dry?

Faustus. Maddening and intolerable thought, that the noble and ethereal part of man must expiate the sins of a body formed of clay!

The devils laughed till the vaults reëchoed.

Satan. Bravo, Faustus! I am convinced, from thy words and behaviour, that thou art too good for a man. I am, besides, much indebted to thee for having invented Printing, that art which is so singularly useful to us.

Pope. What, a printer! He gave himself out at my court for a gentleman, and won my daughter Lucretia!

Faustus. Silence, proud Spaniard. I paid her richly; and thou wouldst have prostituted thyself to me for a like sum, if I had been one of thine own stamp. My noble invention will sow more good, and will be more profitable to the human race, than all the popes from St. Peter down to thyself.

Satan. Thou art mistaken, Faustus. In the first place, men will rob thee' of the honour of having invented this art.

Faustus. That is worse than damnation.

Satan. Observe now this man: he stands before me, the ruler here, and holds everlasting torments as nothing when compared with the loss of his fame and glory, those chimeras of his overheated brain. In the second place, Faustus, the shades will descend by hundreds of thousands, will fall upon thee, and overwhelm thee with curses, for having converted the little stream which poisoned the human mind into a monstrous flood. I, who am the ruler here, and shall gain by it, am therefore thy debtor; and if thou wilt curse the Eternal, who either could not or would not make thee better, thou shalt escape the torments of this place, and I will make thee a prince of my dark kingdom.

Pope. Let me be the first to curse, O Satan; as a pope, I have an undoubted right to the precedence.

Satan. Observe these men, ye devils, and see

how they outdo ye. No, Pope; thou didst it when thy lips kissed the feet of my Leviathan. Choose, Faustus.

Faustus stepped forward; raging despair was engraven in ·frightful characters on his shadowy face. He —— ! Who can express what he said ?

The devils trembled at his words, and were astonished at his audacity. Since hell first existed, no such stillness had reigned in the dark, frightful kingdom, the abode of eternal misery. Faustus broke it, and required Satan to fulfil his promise.

Satan. Fool! how canst thou imagine that I, ruler of hell, will keep my word, as there is no example of a prince of earth ever having kept his word when he got nothing by so doing ? If thou canst forget that thou art a man, forget not that thou standest before the Devil. My fiendish subjects turned pale at thy temerity; thy horrid words made my firm and imperishable throne tremble; and I thought for a moment that I had risked too much. Away! thy presence makes me uneasy; and thou art a proof that man can do more than the Devil can bear. Drag him, ye fiends, into the most frightful corner; let him there languish in solitude, and madden at the recollection of his deeds, and of this moment, which he can never atone for. Let no shade approach him. Go, thou accursed one, and hover alone and abandoned in that land where neither hope, comfort, nor sleep are found. Those doubts which have tormented thee in life shall for ever gnaw thy soul, and no one shall explain to thee that mystery, the pursuit of which has brought thee here. This is the most painful punishment of all to a philosopher like thee. Drag him away, I repeat; torture him. Seize that Pope, and plunge him into the hottest pool; for their equals are not to be found in hell.

After their departure, Satan said to himself, smiling:

"When men wish to represent any thing abominable, they paint the Devil: let us, therefore, in revenge, when we wish to represent any thing infamous, depict man; and philosophers, popes, priests, conquerors, ministers, and authors, shall serve us as models."

CPSIA information can be obtained
at www.ICGtesting.com
Printed in the USA
LVHW040403200422
716646LV00005B/235